ST

Melanie Finn was born and raised in Kenya and educated in the United States. She has lived and worked on four continents as a journalist, screenwriter, ranch hand, documentary film-maker, ski bum and waitress. This is her first novel.

AWAY FROM YOU

When Helen's daughter Ellie returns to her childhood home in Kenya on her father's death after twenty-five years away, it means facing the past. Her upbringing in colonial Africa — stiff whiskies, keeping up appearances and English gardens amidst the African Bush — was marked by a violent father she didn't really know. Yet Ellie is determined to find out the truth about her family ghosts — what was her father's dark secret, and will the truth finally free her from the past?

MELANIE FINN

AWAY
FROM YOU

Complete and Unabridged

ULVERSCROFT
Leicester

First published in Great Britain in 2004 by
Penguin Books
London

First Large Print Edition
published 2005
by arrangement with
The Penguin Group
London

British Library CIP Data

Finn, Melanie
    Away from you.—Large print ed.—
    Ulverscroft large print series: general fiction
    1. Fathers and daughters—Fiction
    2. Kenya—Social life and customs—Fiction
    2. Large type books
    I. Title
    823.9'2 [F]

    ISBN 1–84395–737–X

Published by
F. A. Thorpe (Publishing)
Anstey, Leicestershire

Set by Words & Graphics Ltd.
Anstey, Leicestershire
Printed and bound in Great Britain by
T. J. International Ltd., Padstow, Cornwall

This book is printed on acid-free paper

For my mother and Pop
And in memory of Pascal Privat

Acknowledgements

There are very many people to whom I am deeply grateful. Some, whose names I never knew, collaborated with their kindness: waitresses, women selling trinkets, fellow bus passengers who shared oranges, bus seats and conversations. What they gave got me by.

Those I do know: James and Joyce Finn, Angie and Jonathan Scott, Vanessa Strong, Vivienne North, Joan and David Coward, David Raffman, Trail Boss Gary Suppes, the staff of Maasai Camp, Menina, Jack McCabe, Ernie and Carole Kester, Anne Adams, Martha Mannheim, Jane Carpenter, Emilio and Lupo Santasillia, Matthew Aeberhard, Ian and Jessica Mackichan, my agent Kate Shaw and editor Juliet Annan. Tim Lott, you especially. And my mother and Pop for forwarding my mail, for harassing anyone who owed me money, for the bad jokes, newspaper clippings and sheep shit, for your faith and love: all indispensable.

This is what you remember about him: not much, but then you have been assiduous in your forgetting. His red sweater, v-neck cashmere; the clink of ice cubes in a glass. He is shadow and voice, but you cannot recall his face. He is behind a closed door, in a forbidden room. He is asleep in his armchair, he is asleep in the driveway, asleep in your sandpit, face down, snoring but not harmless, even then. He is shouting, he is whispering, he is close but also remote as if at the end of a long hallway and you cannot hear him. His words never make any sense, he speaks some other language. His hands sometimes spin away from him like windmills, like pinwheels and Catherine wheels, snapping like firecrackers. There must be pain, but you cannot feel it.

Your skin bruises like apples.

1

An intake of breath, or less, the fraction of a second it took to place a paw on the road's outer edge, the flexing of tendons up the leg to the taut muscles of the shoulder.

The coyote's winter-thick tawny fur was lit against the night's dense backdrop with such precision Ellie could see individual hairs. Its eyelashes and whiskers. In less than a breath she and the coyote knew: this intersection in time and space had been waiting for them for hours, or even years. Things always connected back.

If she hadn't seen the coyote she could have mistaken the soft bump for a minor pothole and driven on. Even as she looked in her rear-view mirror, she wanted to believe the coyote was bruised but running through the sagebrush to its den in the arroyo, to the greeting of barks and other wet noses, the smell of escape clinging to its fur. Or she wanted to believe the end had been quick, the impact definitive, the coyote old and at the end of its life; perhaps grateful for her intercession.

Instead she saw it spiralling in on itself.

Back broken, it was spinning on two legs, snapping at its useless haunches. A circus trick performed in the red glow of the car's tail lights just for her, an audience of one. She stopped the car and got out.

There was no other traffic, not here on the back road that hemmed the mountains, not on this cold, hard winter night. There were lights in the distance, eight, ten miles away, the old Spanish towns along the Rio Grande, Velarde, Española, the Indian casinos in Pojoaque. No one close at hand to help. Or worse. She knew what happened to women alone on dark roads or drunk in dark bars, how the police found a pale body sprawled on the roadside and how no one in these small towns ever knew anything.

The tyre iron was in the trunk. Ellie felt its weight in her hands. The coyote didn't even see her coming. Its world had funnelled into a pain purer than any other experience of hunger or comfort or warm May sun on soft belly fur.

The first blow only stunned it. On the second it went down, and on the third she heard the skull crack. Like an egg, she thought. The coyote suddenly relaxed and lay down on the tarmac with a kind of relief. Ellie knelt down and stroked it. The rough coat was matted with pinesap, infested with fleas, torn here on a barbed wire fence or the teeth of a rival, but beautiful nonetheless, shot through with hues of pale grey, gold and silver and downy white on the underbelly. Blood pooled around the coyote's head and though she had felt no heartbeat, it blinked one last time and looked ahead as if focused on its next destination.

The night held them there, cushioning them from the rest of the world which moved noisily toward midnight. Somewhere drunks drove home and couples made love or fought and children dreamed. The lights went out in the Super-Walmart in Española and the bands started up in the bars of Santa Fe. But here, Ellie kneeled in the mountain silence with the coyote's warm blood steaming in the cold air. She became aware of the cold, sharp and certain through her wool sweater, and above her the flawless sky bloomed ever outward and away from her.

After a while she picked up the coyote, carried it off the road and laid it gently amongst the juniper and piñon. The act was inevitably weighed with the sacred. She couldn't bear for the fine bones and white teeth to be ground into the tar by careless drivers in pick-ups — for that dishonour. But honour, she knew, meant nothing to the coyote. Only fences, poison bait and speeding cars meant something. And, anyway, *honour*? What honour is left among us? In moving the coyote, she was simply being indulgent, like some ancient priestess who believes the future can be held at bay by chants and the burning of incense. Ritual is to reassure the living, not the dead.

She felt the rough pads of the coyote's paws and wondered at the miles it had travelled, etching lines in the sand or the snow. She wondered at the life it now left behind, the pack that waited at the edge of the woods — they would call out and there would be no reply. She thought about how the Navajos and Hopis know the coyote as the trickster, a creature whose presence unsettles the familiar. A coyote crossing the road is a messenger trailing change.

As she stood and walked back to the car she felt the change coming, her life beginning to shift. But the shift was happening in the synapse before the actual beginning, where there is only instinct like a faint scent travelling miles downwind.

★ ★ ★

She stopped at a Texaco on the main road and washed the coyote's blood from her hands in the ladies' room. Then she drove on to Santa Fe where she lived with Peter. Not 'home', but Peter's house. Which was her attitude not his. He wanted to share his life, his house, with her. When she moved in, he thought she was like other women and so he suggested they buy new furniture together. He plied her with fabric samples and trips to antique stores. But he soon realized she didn't care — no, more than that: she didn't want to step outside herself and partake. And so the garish sofa set inherited a decade ago from his first wife stayed, as did the coffee table and the curtains and the chipped plates. After two years together there was barely a trace of Ellie around the house; only books and half-drunk cups of tea.

Peter's house was at the end of a cul-de-sac of low-slung adobe bungalows ubiquitous in New Mexico. His Chevy Suburban was in the driveway, all manner of tools carefully ordered in the back. He'd left the front hall light on for her but otherwise the house was dark. She knew how he would be sleeping, on his back, baring himself to the world. She knew she would climb in next to him and he would reach for her, his big hands pulling her close to the enormous furnace of his body. From their first night together he had been a windbreak between her and the rest of the world.

Moses, the cat, waited by the front door, indifferent as ever. Peter had got him from the pound, had gone in on Christmas Eve and demanded the animal next in line for gassing. 'We don't gas them,' the volunteer told him, 'We euthanize them by injection.' 'Just give me the damn cat,' Peter had said. And they gave him Moses, who had viciously rejected all overtures of affection ever since.

Ellie let him in, followed him into the kitchen and poured herself a glass of rum, neat — the only spirit she could find in the cabinet by the fridge. On the fridge were photographs, a jigsaw of Peter's life that he carefully compiled and updated. Friends laughing, fishing trips, his nieces building a snowman, Moses stalking mice in the long grass behind the house.

There was a picture of Ellie, caught three-quarter face in the morning light last winter. The wind lifted her dark hair away from her neck, exposing her throat and cheekbones. Behind her, out of focus, was the tawny scrub and marshes of Bosque del Apache. She wasn't looking at the camera, but away from it, laughing, saying, 'Go away! I hate having my picture taken.'

Ellie looked now at a photograph of Peter from years ago, the summer's Kodachrome colours long faded. He was ten, fishing off

Martha's Vineyard with his dad. His dad would say, 'Watch the gulls, they know where the fish are.' And Peter would watch the gulls and cast his line.

This was still how he moved through life, with an eye for the practical, using knowledge and skill to accomplish a definitive goal. He was a builder by profession, which was no different to fishing. Once you understood how the tools worked, the limits of materials, and trusted the steadiness of your hands, there were no surprises. And this was what he was offering her: a close-held life; not predictable but run through with sameness. He would love her always with his big strong healthy heart. He would never leave her.

★   ★   ★

Peter rolled onto his side, cupping her naked body, drawing her in to the sleepy warmth of the bed. Her smell was finally familiar to him, the layers of her like seasons. 'It's late. You've been out driving?'

'I needed to.'

He didn't ask why. There was so little he could explain about her. The driving was the least of it. How she'd drive all over New Mexico, taking I-40 to Gallup or the back road to Jemez or out to the listening station in

Datil. All those hours and miles and no real destination. She just went, sometimes with a map, mostly without. Sometimes she didn't drive far, maybe just to Abiquiu where she'd hike around all day. She loved the fire-coloured rocks, the wind-carved canyons where Georgia O'Keeffe's ghost peered through old cow skulls at the sky.

Peter hoped that one day she might bring him something back, a pebble she'd found in the dust, earth-hued and smooth. Or a story, some funny incident she'd witnessed in a coffee shop in Socorro or Madrid. To share might be an act of staying. He waited for such an event, patiently and because there was no alternative. She'd come to him trailing her different pasts behind her like ribbons on a kite. She'd been long legs and bravado, with a couple of suitcases and a stack of driver's licences from a dozen states. She'd leave just the same way. Sometimes he fooled himself it would be different, that he could make her stay. Love gives you all kinds of delusions.

'And you?' she said. 'Did the plumber finally show?'

He laughed softly in the dark. 'His sister had a baby, so he says tomorrow. Without fail.'

'I thought his sister had a baby last week.'

'That was his wife.'

'How many more babies might there be?'

'Oh, I think they've all been born. But now, you see, they can get sick and will have to be taken to the hospital.'

'You should just hire someone else. An orphan, someone with no family, a social outcast with no friends.'

'I should,' he said. But they both knew he wouldn't. Even though the plumber had failed to show up at the job-site for three weeks, Peter wouldn't fire him. He was faithful to those most faithless, he considered it payback to the world for all the fine things that had been laid upon his table. This she respected in him most of all, this rare gift to acknowledge the bounty of his life.

Now his hand slid across her hip to the curve of her waist. She knew the sign language and replied, softening toward him. He traced her collarbones with his carpenter's hands, admiring the joists, the deceptively delicate frame of her. He kissed all her sharp angles and smooth planes.

'Eleanor,' he whispered, and she leaned forward to kiss him, her hair covering their faces like a hide.

2

The letter came in the mail the next day, with the phone bill, a bank statement and a sale flyer from Vons supermarket. She knew the coyote hadn't brought it — she didn't believe in magic, only in symbols. But she wondered. How things are connected.

She knew where it came from by the stamp, a bright exotic bird whose name she'd long forgotten. She opened the cream-coloured envelope, the heavy, formal bond favoured by lawyers everywhere. And she read the letter.

What should she feel?

Certainly not grief. She hadn't thought of him for years, he was dead to her already. She wanted nothing to do with him, even dead in a letter.

Or the country. Forsaken long ago, it was now someone else's fantasy, a destination for package tours and Peace Corps workers.

The car keys were in her hand already, and so she drove north, past Española, turning right, and found herself where she had been the night before. A bus-load of school children drove by, their noise like a radio tuning in and out.

She got out of the car and sat on the hood. She could see and hear through the trees that a murder of crows had descended upon the coyote. She could not fault their lascivious cawing, how they fluttered and strutted in their widow's cloaks. Here, beyond man, death was always good for something. Death strung lives together like pearls.

The winter sun was brassy and hard and from the low-angled light there was no reprieve. She squinted, looking out across the landscape. The beauty had held her here far longer than any other place. The high peaks of the Sangre de Cristos hurried down to plains of sagebrush. In the west rose Mount Taylor and the solid monolith of the Pedernal where the sunset danced. Between here and there lay the Rio Grande and all manner of tributaries lined with willow and Spanish olive, aspen and oak; the irrigated orchards and hay fields; the crumbling houses the colour of earth. And above, always, the vast sky that left nowhere to hide.

She would be gone by the time Peter got home. This was how she left her other lovers, her other cities. She had perfected the art of leaving but not of farewell. After all, what was there to say? 'I don't love you. The failing is mine. The plumber can't come on time and I can't love, that's all there is to it, and every day with you reminds me of my failing.' Or worse: 'I'm sorry,' as if any apology, ever, was adequate. And she wasn't sorry, she wasn't filled with sorrow, she wasn't anything. She was light as a moth fluttering away.

★   ★   ★

Three days' driving and Ellie was there, the dirt road through the Maine woods where spring waited in the trees' tight buds, and across the wooden bridge that connected the rest of the world to Heron Island. The dogs came running out, barking, wagging their tails. Four dogs now, Ellie noticed. One up from last time — and this one, odds-on, also a stray.

The house was a summer cabin that Gus had winterized himself. Before retirement he'd been a businessman with soft, inept hands. He'd learned the hard way about toilets and water pumps and damp rot. The lights were on against an early dusk. There was smoke from the chimney.

Gus came out in the freezing wind. 'Ellie?'

'I should have phoned.' She stepped out of the car.

He was smiling, moving toward her in a tussle of dog. 'It's a wonderful surprise. It's great.'

As he hugged her, she realized he was old. Frailness had set in, a new thinness to his body under his heavy work shirts and rugged boots. Five years ago when she had been here last he had seemed ageless, a potent man still in the middle of his life. But of course, even then he'd been seventy.

He insisted on carrying her suitcase. It wasn't heavy but she could see it was an effort. Though not as much of an effort, perhaps, as to admit he couldn't carry it.

'Your mother'll be happy to see you. She's a bit under the weather. A bad cold she picked up from the school.'

'All those kids with snotty noses.'

'She works too hard. She wears herself down. People lean on her too much.'

'She does exactly what she wants to do. No one forces her to volunteer at the library. Or whatever it is.' Ellie was careful to keep the accusation out of her voice. But the anger was there again — always — a hard tumour at the base of her throat.

'The children's library, adult literacy in the prison, and all her usual lame ducks. Last week Rachel's husband just left her so we have Rachel on the phone, Rachel around for tea, Rachel around for coffee. They wear her down.'

It was always like this, Gus as her mother's protector. As if her mother was some guileless, delicate creature the rest of the world used as a doormat. Always. Ellie remembered something Peter said: Some things in life are certain; death, taxes and that your family will piss you off. He said other things, one-liners that made her laugh out loud. Once, she'd dragged him to a Japanese movie. The subtitles came up and he said, 'Gee, sweetie, if I'd wanted to read I would've stayed home with a book.'

Gus pulled open the front door and they edged by the woodpile that crowded the mudroom. 'This is the last winter we're going to have the stove. Your mother hates it. We'll switch to propane now.'

The dogs rushed inside with them, a current of noise and fur. 'Helen?' Gus called out.

But she was already coming into the kitchen, a petite, fine-boned woman with short hair that was still thick and dark, though shot through with pure white. She put her arms around Ellie. She smelt of Oil of Olay and cough drops. 'This is such a lovely surprise.'

'It's just for the night. Is it all right if I leave

my car here?' Ellie knew there would be questions — where and why — but her mother would wait and then ask them casually, as if they had just occurred to her, as if the answers didn't matter.

'Of course,' Helen said. 'Come on, I'll put the kettle on. You want tea or coffee, or herb tea? Mint, chamomile? Are you hungry? I've got lemon cake.'

★ ★ ★

Helen was a good cook. She made roast lamb for dinner with rosemary and homemade mint jelly. In addition to everything else she did she made jellies and jams and pickles with goods from her garden and from the woods.

'So, how's New Mexico?' Helen handed Ellie a plate. The questions had begun.

'It's fine.'

'Gus and I thought you might settle there.'

'I'm not sure.'

'Is it Peter? Did things go wrong?'

Ellie looked at her mother. 'Why I'm here, Mum, isn't anything to do with Peter. John died.'

For a moment Helen didn't understand. Then she took in a breath. 'Oh. When?'

'A few months ago. I don't know any details.'

Helen turned her head away. Gus put his hand on hers. 'Poor man,' she said. 'Poor bastard.'

This was the first they had spoken of him in more than twenty years. And this was her mother's contribution. Poor man, poor bastard.

Ellie said, 'The lawyer suggested I go out there to take care of the will. I don't have to, I could do it by FedEx, but he said it was 'preferable'.'

'Who is the lawyer?'

'Richard Boudreau.'

Helen leaned back. 'Dickie B. So he's still around.'

★   ★   ★

Later, Ellie lay in bed in the guest room. She had no room of her own in this house as Gus and her mother had moved up here a decade ago. By then, Ellie was miles away. There was nothing of hers here, even though Helen had tried. She'd packed up Ellie's things in the old house in Connecticut, teenage girls' things, books, posters, records, some old clothes, but Ellie had never claimed them. Helen eventually took them to the thrift store.

'Ellie?' Helen tapped softly on the door.

18

'Are you awake?' She sneezed as she entered and retrieved a Kleenex from her dressing gown. 'Damn this cold.' She sat on the edge of the bed. 'I know you don't want to talk about it.'

Ellie said, 'I just didn't want to tell you on the phone. He was your husband for ten years.'

'And your father.'

No, Ellie thought, my father only for the moment of conception. She said instead, 'Besides, the flights from Boston are cheaper.'

Helen looked down. 'I'm glad you came. For whatever reason.' She stroked the bedspread, picking up a loose thread. 'I feel ... I don't know, it's so long ago. Sad, I guess, but a sadness that's old and worn out, a sort of memory of how sad I was that it didn't work out for us. Not really for his death. He wasn't a young man. He's had his life.'

Ellie said, 'My flight's at noon. Can you or Gus take me to the shuttle?'

'Of course, of course,' Helen squeezed Ellie's hand. 'I wish you were staying for longer.' She stood quickly; the touch had broken the protocol between them. 'Gus and I were thinking we could come and visit if you went back to New Mexico. He's always wanted to go to the southwest, Tucson,

Flagstaff, the Grand Canyon.'

'That's Arizona.'

'Well, it's all the same, isn't it? Cowboys and adobe.'

Of course it's not the same. Ellie looked up at her mother. Helen was trying so hard to breach the distance between them. But the distance was infinite, the distance was years and years.

Helen put her hand in her pocket and drew out an envelope. 'I found this in my desk. It's all that's left. Keep it if you want. Otherwise, throw it away. I couldn't bring myself to do that even though it's nothing to do with me any more.'

It was a photograph, faded brown and white, of a small, thin boy standing with a woman on the dock of a tropical port. The boy frowns — or is he squinting at the sun? And the woman smiles, but not convincingly. On the back is written: 'Dar es Salaam 1928.'

'They sent him away when he was very little,' Helen said. 'I think that's when it started, his moving away from the world.' She fussed with a button on her dressing gown. 'But who knows. It doesn't matter now.'

She brushed a stray strand of hair away from Ellie's face. 'I won't kiss you, not with this cold. But sleep tight. See you in the morning.' She stood up and closed the door behind her.

Ellie looked again at the picture. How odd, she thought, to see John Cameron so small and vulnerable, so unsure, just a thin boy being sent away. Was this the starting point as her mother had said? But where and when do our lives start? Not heart and lungs but dreams and choices. When does the damage begin?

Here, a small boy waited for a ship, for a wife and a daughter. For a mistress. For whisky, for hurting. For killing. Ellie put the photograph face down on the table beside the bed. The traces of him in her mind, the whispers. Close her eyes and she could still see his hand moving like electricity through the air, the slap and the shame burning together. Pouring whisky the way he liked it, the way he'd taught her, but there was never praise. There was silence, shut-up, be-quiet, knock-it-off, go-to-your-room. And there was Mrs McMullen with the belt around her neck, the veins on her legs, her bulging dead eyes.

All this is waiting out there for a small boy.

3

It was 1961. Aunt B and Uncle Stanley had a sugar estate in Jinja, forty miles east of Kampala on the edge of Lake Victoria, right at the source of the Nile. There was a little plaque commemorating Speke's discovery a century before.

Uganda was still the Pearl of Africa then. Life was good, the sugar business prosperous, as were cotton, tea, coffee and tourism. The mild air, the strong seasons of wet and dry, the friendly natives, the fertile earth — to the Wickses it was paradise. And home, for they had forfeited England and the dark, cold days where the future held nothing more than a walk to the corner shop for the newspaper and a pint of milk.

After the Second World War, they'd boarded a ship in Southampton and never looked back. Stanley worked his way up in the business until he was a partner with Nile Sugar Industries. They lived in the big house on the hill now, not one of the bungalows on the lowland in a fog of mosquitoes. Their house was cool and filled with white-coated servants who turned down beds, polished the silver and served cocktails with limes from the kitchen garden.

It was B's idea that Helen should come out from England and stay, to give her a chance to recover after that unpleasant business with her fiancé, and maybe, who knows, find another young man here. There were plenty about.

For Helen her first desire had been escape. She hadn't loved Charlie but she was humiliated. She wondered if a broken heart could possibly hurt more than broken pride. She could no longer stand the sympathetic looks, the pity dates — the neighbour's sister's son, the village parson's cousin — lined up for her at tea or Sunday lunch. People treated her like a cracked cup, something that needed careful handling and was no longer of use for 'best'. The truth was that Charlie had left her — for a fat girl with a loud voice and a lot of money — not because Helen was less than perfect. She was fine-limbed, smooth-skinned, pretty by any standards. Lilac was a colour she wore particularly well. But she knew, too, that she had been dispossessed of her future, and there was nothing in England for her anymore.

When she had completed her typing course, she flew to Entebbe on BOAC. Her parents paid — the only money they would ever give her. It wasn't that they wanted to get rid of her, just that they hadn't planned on having her around, an unmarried daughter, nearly twenty-four. What would they do with her? Helen hated flying but even in her fear she looked out the window at the stars. She was among them now, another light in the sky that an African might look up from his hut and see.

Just before landing, the plane broke through the cloud and Helen saw the lake and green hills. Everything seemed new, freshly grown, unruly. It had not been manicured by man, shaped, trimmed, cut. No tidy hedgerows or clipped wheat fields but a tangled green jungle that tumbled into the lake. Here was nature without manners.

Aunt B and Uncle Stanley were there to greet her. She hadn't seen them since she was a child but they seemed no different from her memory. Or perhaps they just looked as she'd expected: a middle-aged, middle-class couple in colonial Africa. Aunt B in a sturdy frock that was well out of fashion, Stanley in khaki shorts, knee socks and safari boots. With them was a Yorkshire terrier, and outside, an old Mercedes and a driver, Sampson. Helen could not help sneaking looks at Sampson as they drove back to Jinja. He was black as coal, blacker than she imagined a black man could be. She wondered that skin could be such a solid, fathomless tone, not vague and opalescent like white skin.

She settled right in. She sometimes wondered at the perfection she was experiencing, the ease of movement and being, her cotton dress swirling about her legs, the morning breeze off the lake. Surely she was entitled to it. She was a good person, helpful, well behaved. She believed in an Episcopalian fate: that if you were good, fate was kind. After all, fate had guided her here, just as fate had made Charlie a greedy, inadequate man whom she was well rid of. He had met his future wife at a party which Helen, sick with flu, had been unable to attend with him. Fate again. Good riddance, she thought; although she secretly hoped that he'd hear of her adventures through mutual friends and rue his choice.

In the mornings, over tea and grapefruit, she read Daphne Du Maurier — all that dark mystery and high windows and secret love. Then she walked down the hill, a quarter of a mile or so, to the estate office. Here, Stanley coped with the daily dramas. Machines broke, diesel ran low or out, the foreman was sick — or drunk. She had her own office, a desk and a chair, a calendar from the Uganda

Sugar Board. It was menial work, typing and filing, letters and forms. Anywhere but here she would have been bored to tears. But from her window she could see the sun shift in the courtyard, a mongoose sniffing the air, birds like bright ribbons.

After work, she would take one of the horses and ride down to the lake through a landscape so fertile you could put a twig in the ground and a few weeks later find a tree. The red earth was so moist, so alive. Uncle Stanley said he was sure he could hear it talking, whispering. What would that earth have to say now? What would the hundred thousand skulls buried in the cane fields tell us?

But then, back then, before the massacres by Milton Obote and Idi Amin, there were jacarandas and sunbirds along the path to the lake, and everything was green, deep, damp emerald green and rustling. The tall grass brushed against Helen's long legs as she rode and soaked the cotton of her jodhpurs and polished the horse's bay flanks. The lake would come to her in streaks of blue through the trees with its strong, dark, water smell.

At the water's edge, Africans would be fishing or doing their washing or collecting water in old petrol cans. The women sang softly and the men made no sound but for the soft splash of their lines in the water. They nodded and smiled as Helen passed, 'Memsahib.'

The lake was endless and opaque, utterly still, a platter of blue. It stretched miles and miles south, somewhere to the sky. Helen's heart felt open in her chest. She was content and sure that things would work out for her. She would fall in love with a wonderful man and live without regret. He was out there. The lake was her Frenchman's Creek.

Then she'd turn back to the stables, a slow canter back up the path through the cool, oozing shadows and around the stable gates just in time, for on the equator the sun snaps shut like a blind; there is darkness in an instant. As soon as she walked in the doors of the house, Ojok, the houseboy, handed her a brandy and soda. She sat on the sofa reading letters from England that told of strikes and bad weather, the price of eggs and beef. She smiled and thought of mangoes, how her friends would never know the taste or the colour of the skin like a sunrise.

★ ★ ★

Aunt B and Uncle Stanley led an active social life. There were frequent cocktail parties, luncheons, and 'do's'. The parties were an antidote to the boredom of living in a country without music, theatre or cinemas (one attended the amateur attempts in Kampala out of sheer camaraderie — certainly not for entertainment — unless one found public humiliation amusing). But the parties were tedious, for there was seldom anything new to talk about. Even the complaints were always the same: the clumsiness of servants, the stupidity of Africans, the shortage of butter or candles or paraffin.

Occasionally, there was real scandal: an affair, a bankruptcy or divorce. Mostly, however, the gossip was petty — members of the community behaving in a manner inappropriate to their station, a catalogue of slights and unbecoming behaviour. James Alton swearing on the tennis court. Peggy Mitcham passing out drunk at the Morris's Christmas party. It was said she vomited as well. Royal Club of Jinja members who had not paid their bar chits, who parked in the Chairman's parking space, who suggested Ugandans or Asians be allowed to join, or at least dine in the club restaurant. The rules were both written and unwritten, and someone was always watching, noting, whispering behind a cupped hand.

Helen had at first imagined that the claustrophobia of small-town England, of

Bibury, Burwash and Epsom Downs, could not exist in Tororo, Kakindi, Tank Hill. But she came to see how the landscape, map-less and unbounded, frightened people and drew them together in clutches. They marked lines and divisions amongst themselves because they could not mark the wilful land. They enforced rules amongst each other because the natives wouldn't obey them, the natives defied domestication. For instance, if one taught one's houseboy how to pour beer on Tuesday, by Wednesday he would have forgotten.

Helen observed this over the course of her time in Uganda. But as she was never tempted to disobey the rules, to swear or drink or plunder someone else's marriage, the rules did not constrain her. Rules don't apply until they are broken.

A week after she arrived, the Wickses received a lunch invitation from Lady Elizabeth Dennett and her husband Simon. The Dennetts were the top of the heap — even though there were perennial rumours about his solvency. In Uganda they were without peer and were thus reduced to socializing with those far below their rank. But they did so with casual *noblesse oblige*. Aunt B was initially ecstatic about the invitation from 'darling Lizzie', but then she realized there was the question of Helen, who could not be left home alone. Yet she could hardly tag along.

Stanley said, 'Just call her, for Christ's sake, tell her about Helen.' This only revealed Stanley's boorishness, a quality B did her best to ignore in private and disguise in public.

'I can't just call her and *invite* my niece. Lizzie may well have a complicated table plan, the numbers will be all wrong,' B explained, although she shouldn't have had to explain, it was so bleeding obvious.

After strenuous consultation with Marge Alton, B decided to send Helen in her place. In the end, this didn't happen because Elizabeth sent another invitation for Helen, having heard on the grapevine about the new arrival.

The Dennetts lived on the Kampala side of Jinja on a bluff overlooking the Sese Islands on Victoria. It was a smaller house than one would expect, but exquisitely decorated. Elizabeth had such taste and style, and many of the antiques were her family heirlooms: a darling Davenport desk, a set of hunting prints.

Simon Dennett had a patrician handsomeness, a classic nose, a tall, lean frame on which to hang his tailored safari suits — tailored, mind you, not by some local

Indian chappie, but by his father's tailor in London. Simon was Savile Row safari.

Elizabeth was a fragile beauty, dark-haired and cream-skinned. She talked of Ascot and dinner at Claridge's. She wore Hermès scarves with reckless abandon and had once even wiped up a coffee spill with one. But it wasn't pretence with Elizabeth. She had natural grace, a neck like a swan, and arching vowels.

She was mindful of Helen and flattered her in the seating plan by placing her next to Simon at the head of the table. Helen minded her manners and listened. There was talk about the Mau Mau uprising in Kenya.

Even though the worst of it had happened in the mid-fifties, those at the table brought out the stories again and again, as if to remind themselves of the savagery of Africans, to remind themselves never to be lulled by the beauty of the continent and the smiles of their servants.

Helen listened but could not connect her experience of Africa with what she heard: men tied to stakes and covered in honey so the safari ants would slowly eat them to death, babies with their heads smashed in — *white* babies. *By their ayahs.*

'Our blacks aren't like that,' said a woman in a mauve dress across the table. 'This is

31

Uganda, not Kenya. The Baganda had a real civilization before we came. They're a gentle people.'

Simon Dennett laughed, 'A gentle people? The Kabaka used to decorate his house with human heads.' Elizabeth was looking at him, Helen could see, her elegant fingers tensing on the butter knife. Simon went on, '*Our* blacks would cut our throats in a second, and in half a second they'd cut each other's throats. They're good at killing. They don't have to count it or turn it on or polish it, they can just kill. Killing is like breaking things. Whoops, your head is gone, *pole sana*. So sorry! Plus,' he stabbed a piece of roast beef with his fork, pinned it to the table, 'They have a tremendous aptitude for dying.'

There was silence. His lips were wine-stained and he'd drunk too much. Elizabeth said, 'Well, thank you for that, darling.' And then, in a firm voice, drawing all eyes to her like a puppeteer: 'The Russians have put a man in space. I heard it on the World Service this morning. Rather shows our side up, don't you think?' And that was the end of the stories about the Mau Mau.

After lunch, the men went outside to urinate in the flowerbed. There was only one toilet in the house and naturally it was reserved for the women. But while the men stood equably, side by side, chatting away, the women had to queue. Helen noticed how they arranged themselves, ever-so-politely and effortlessly, an unspoken choreography, in accordance with rank. Aunt B knew she was behind Rosemary Beauford, whose husband was the vice-consul, but ahead of Mary Chambers, whose husband worked for Barclays Bank. Lavinia O'Malley went last, being Catholic, Irish and the wife of a schoolteacher.

Over coffee, served by a tall silent African in a white kanzu, Helen felt Elizabeth looking at her. She flushed involuntarily and glanced up. 'Such a fresh face,' said Elizabeth. 'Such wide eyes.' Then she stared out across her perfectly manicured lawn to the lake as it melted into the afternoon heat. 'Africa hasn't sunk her teeth into you yet.' And Helen didn't understand — was this a compliment? Or a warning?

Then Elizabeth said, 'He's Pokot,' and gestured to her servant. 'They're a wild tribe in the north, they don't wear clothing, just spears and jewellery. Very sexual, don't you think?' Helen looked at him, but only briefly, because she didn't want to think of him naked. All that uninterrupted blackness frightened her a little.

At three it was time to leave, the guests

giving thanks and kisses in the same order of ascendance in which they'd queued for the toilet. Simon walked the Wickses and Helen out to their car. He shook Stanley's hand, kissed Aunt B. And kissed Helen. His hand lingered for a moment on her lower back. She couldn't be sure if she felt a slight pressure in his touch, as if he was either moving her forward or holding her back. But a pressure — surely? — a warmth that floated down through the silk of her dress and rested on her bare skin. As she moved away she saw Elizabeth standing in the front doorway, raising her white hand in a languid wave.

They drove away. Aunt B said, 'Simon walked us to the car, did you notice? He's never done that before.' She glanced at Helen, unknowing and unconcerned, a dark curl coming loose from her chignon. And B knew there would be no more invitations to the Dennetts as long as pretty Helen was around.

* * *

Within a fortnight, Helen had met every eligible young man in the country. There was Niall, a captain with the police force in Kampala. James, secretary at the High Commission. Rupert, a game warden in

Murchison Falls National Park. Henry, the agent for an import-export firm. And David, a mathematics teacher at the university. There were others, but Aunt B was scrupulous. Suitors with imperfect manners, the wrong accent, or liberal views regarding the indigenous population were quickly culled. Harold made the tragic error of referring to napkins as 'serviettes'. Another young man with promising credentials (an uncle with a knighthood) said he believed in the right of self-determination for all mankind.

Uncle Stanley couldn't contain himself. 'What? Giving the vote to the bloody munts?'

'Stanley!' said Aunt B.

'They did it in America a century ago,' said the young man.

'But they weren't serious,' countered Uncle Stanley.

'Oh, I think they're getting serious now.'

There was a terrible hush at the table. Aunt B said, 'More vegetables?'

The young man was never seen again.

Briefly, Rupert was a strong contender. He arranged for an extravagant weekend camping trip to Murchison Falls, collecting Helen in a convoy of three Land Rovers. Helen watched the tatty outskirts of Kampala yield to jungle, the good, wide road become a narrow track through trees and vines. From the roaming green came bush-buck and diker that panicked in the brief sunlight, as if caught naked. There were Colobus monkeys in the canopy above, flashing their white tails, half jumping, half flying from branch to branch. And along the roadside, troops of baboons stared at the cars, low-browed and swaggering.

I'm here, this is me, Helen thought, on safari in Africa. She was glamorous, Grace Kelly in a silk headscarf. She could see herself making wildlife documentaries, having a cheetah as a pet, working with lions.

They passed through villages that stuttered out of the jungle. Flocks of naked children ran alongside the car smiling and waving, in the days before they yelled out 'Give me money!' or 'Give me sweetie.' The days before so many of them would be dead from AIDS, Ebola, politics.

By lunchtime they'd arrived at a clearing by the river, not far from the falls. Rupert took her on a game drive while the staff set up camp. She saw elephant, giraffe, lion, zebra, rhino. She saw herds of buffalo and took Rupert's lead in calling them 'buff'. She stood below the falls themselves, the spray falling on her like a baptism. By dusk, when they returned, a shower with hot water had been erected for her behind a canvas screen.

The silver candelabras were lit and a dinner of duck à l'orange was served. In the darkness, the hyrax screamed and the bush seethed with sound: grunts, rustles, roars. Rupert said that if Helen was afraid of sleeping alone he could move his camp bed into her tent. Or even right outside it. Politely, she demurred — she truly wasn't afraid.

Later, she heard him outside her tent, pacing and pacing and sighing softly. He declared his love for her the next day as they watched a pride of lion sleep in the narrow noon shade. It was a supremely romantic moment, but there was no avoiding the tinyness of Rupert's hands: those pale, feminine extremities were like roots or bulbs grown in the dark. Helen could not imagine them touching her.

Then there was Henry. He had a dusty little second-floor office in Kampala from which he exported tea. In the courtyard below him an Indian spice business thrived, and so Henry's office, and even Henry himself, always smelled vaguely of cardamom and cloves.

Often, when meeting him for lunch, Helen would come early so she could wait in the open walkway on a wooden chair and observe the world below. There floated the dark-skinned women in saris who ran the business from behind their account books. Their men folk shouted at each other and shunted the sacks of spices from one corner of the courtyard to the other. Children ran loose and loud, and the sunlight was littered with incense and particles of spice.

Henry would emerge and apologize for the 'Bloody, dirty Pakis,' though, if he'd cared to ask, he would have found they were not from Pakistan, but from Goa. He escorted Helen up the street to the Embassy Hotel for a buffet lunch. As they ate, he would tell her in detail about his mother's flower garden at home in Kent.

Sensing she was growing bored with him (and what a feat of male insight that had been) he took her to the Black Cat, a nightclub in the heart of Kampala. In the crowded, smoky depths, blacks and whites mingled freely. And more. As the Congolese band pounded out Nat King Cole, Helen saw a white man with his hands on the swaying hips of a Ugandan girl, how he pushed her away from him, then close, turning her, dipping her, how her breasts strained against her pink top. They danced fiercely, more an exorcism than a samba. Helen watched her sweat-shining skin and her muscles rippling and the boneless movements of her body.

Henry saw Helen staring. 'Disgusting, isn't it? I don't know why they let them in here.'

'Who?' she said.

'The tarts.'

'I thought she was . . . dancing, just having a good time.'

Henry laughed, but gently, indulgently. 'I suppose you don't see that sort of thing in England, not a nice girl like you. I'm sorry to shock you.'

Helen drank her vodka and passionfruit juice. Henry was wrong. Even if the girl was a tart, she was still a dancer, she was still having a good time. She was more than the money she was paid. Henry, on the other hand, was just a bore.

Over cups of tea, she and Aunt B giggled about these encounters, these men with their fumbling desires. And then B would pat Helen's hand and say, 'Don't worry, dear. The right one will come along.'

Helen wasn't worried. He would find her.

4

There was turbulence over the Rift Valley.
The plane dropped and skipped as it topped
the western slopes of the Ngong Hills. A
woman passenger somewhere let out a little
squeal. Ellie asked the African businessman
sitting next to her if she could hold his hand.
He smiled kindly and said 'Of course,' even
though they hadn't said a word to each other
since London.

'You're like my wife,' he said. 'She hates to
fly.'

To Ellie it was more than the flying, placing
herself at the mercy of some ego-merchant in
the cockpit. For the first time in her life she
was going backward instead of forward.
Ahead of her was the past, not some nameless
city circled on the map, she in her getaway
car heading into the night and a safe new
future.

What she loved about America was the
choice of futures: so many destinations and
each one a different life. You could leave Salt
Lake and be in San Francisco the next day,
be a receptionist in Los Angeles or a waitress
in Santa Fe. It was a country of reinvention,

where the past didn't matter and no one bothered with it. They barely taught history in the schools. It was the land of opportunity and those moving forward, driven by their own internal manifest destiny, knew you travelled farthest if you travelled lightest. You left your past on Ellis Island or in a Greyhound bus terminal. Or in a dozen rented rooms. Or pinned to a lover's fridge door.

Once, her mother had said to her, 'Why are you always moving? What are you looking for?'

This was a familiar accusation. That in moving, she was looking for or running away from something.

She had replied, 'And staying is better?'

Helen, who had stayed, who had stayed too long, had said nothing more.

Ellie's hand rested lightly in the African's hand. When the plane dipped again, she gave it an involuntary squeeze. He laughed and said, 'My wife leaves me with bruises.'

He was a heavy-set man with very dark skin. He wore a gold Rolex, jeans, sneakers and a Florida State sweatshirt. But for his slight accent he could have been an African-American, or a second-generation Brit.

'Are you on safari?' he asked her.

'Business,' she said.

'Your first time here?'

She hesitated, not wanting the conversation, but not wanting to be rude. 'I was born here.'

'Really. And what did your parents do?'

'My father was an accountant.'

'But they left?'

'Yes.' The easiest explanation, not the truth.

'Bad times,' he said, then forced a posh English accent: 'Not like the good old days, eh? Before Independence.'

He laughed without humour. 'When you were our masters and could do whatever you wanted. An army of white people marching like ants across our land, getting into everything, every corner, every little crack. Only not like ants because you had your laws and your bible. Do you know what Mzee Kenyatta said? You gave us your bible and taught us to read but when we looked up from the bible you had taken our land. Your mother, I can imagine, a real memsahib. Did she shout at the servants? 'Lete gin and tonic haraka!' Suddenly she is a duchess! And your father, stealing from us, one set of accounts for his clients, another for the government. Very pukha!'

His vehemence surprised her. She withdrew her hand.

'I don't remember,' she said. But there had

42

been the servants' quarters behind the house, the small, dark rooms, the single, cold tap, and Rosa who couldn't read or write. She signed her pay slips with an 'X'.

The flight steward announced preparations for landing.

The African reached over and put his hand on hers for a moment. 'I'm sorry. I've been rude. I'm worried about things. My mother. I've taken her for medical treatment to England because what she needs isn't available here. Here, at the government hospital, the doctors haven't been paid for three months. Inside it's shameful — rats and faeces, people lying in the hallways, dying or dead, who can tell. I think to myself, 'This is the best we can do for ourselves?' ' He shrugged. 'And anyway, better you British than the Belgians. Look at the Congo. They cut off their hands. Or Ethiopia. The Italians left them with only pretty buildings and cappuccino machines.'

The plane hit the runway. Out the window Ellie saw dry grass, the grey cement airport building. When the plane came to a stop, there was the usual rush for belongings and the door. After he'd collected his bag from the overhead locker, the African handed her his card. Printed on expensive stock: Julius P. Mwangi, Esquire. Attorney-at-law.

'You never know when you might need a lawyer,' he said and smiled, trying to make up for earlier.

She filed along with the other passengers and stepped out into the jet-fuelled air, down the metal staircase and onto the tarmac. She was here, now, after twenty-five years. The ground beneath her feet held her, but the stewardess was urging everyone into the building. She had no choice but to carry on, shuffling obediently with the others, drugged by boredom, bad food and free booze. A flannel-grey sky had lowered itself onto the earth, closing the planet off from the universe, locking in the human race. Everything felt heavy, weighted by gravity.

And she knew that she shouldn't have come back.

★ ★ ★

At the baggage carousel she saw Julius Mwangi again. He was waving to his wife and small children who waited on the other side of a grubby glass partition in the arrivals hall. His fat wife wore a Chanel-style suit, her little hippo feet stuffed into high heels. The children, two girls, two boys, were wearing frilly dresses or jeans. Julius caught Ellie's eye and smiled, 'I am a lucky man.'

44

And he was, for his luggage came out first. He spoke to a porter in abrupt English: 'Be careful, you fool! Hurry up!' The porter, a small man, his white-haired head atop a thin neck, was clearly too old for this kind of work and struggled with the trio of vast suitcases.

In passing, Julius said: 'Be careful here. There are thieves everywhere. These people are all thieves.' He smiled his goodbye, then, turning, berated the ancient porter for his stupidity and slowness, and was gone, waved through customs by smiling officials.

While Ellie waited for her own suitcase, she looked around at the airport, which had opened a year before she left. It was now shabby and disordered. Three international flights had arrived at once, and all were using the same baggage carousel — the only one of five that worked. In the far corner, perhaps a hundred unclaimed suitcases were stacked against the wall. How long had they been there?

At the customs counters, several passengers — all Asians, she noticed — were opening their suitcases for inspection. Customs officials pulled out the contents with the barely restrained glee of children at Christmas. Mostly, they found only clothes — bras and pyjamas — but occasionally a Sony

Discman, a bottle of undeclared brandy, computer games. These were duly confiscated.

There was a shortage of trolleys with operable wheels, so passengers dragged their belongings like carcasses across a floor littered with cigarette butts, sweet wrappers and brown spots of what may have been chewing gum. Thick-limbed Americans with vast backpacks and open-toed sandals, a group of Italian tourists wearing name-tags and smoking furiously (no one paid attention to the 'Smoking Prohibited' signs), Africans with battered cardboard boxes tied up with sisal rope — whatever noise any of them might have generated was drowned by the clanking and moaning of the baggage carousel.

Ellie found her suitcase and waded through the crowd and out into the arrivals hall. A group of school children with earnest faces and pressed uniforms was singing a welcome song for their returning teacher. Arab women in black shifts waved frantically through the glass at a group of men in white robes who'd come off the Yemeni flight from Sana'a. Beyond them stood a man in a cream-coloured safari suit with her name on a hotel sign. She nodded at him.

'Jambo, Miss Cameroon,' he said with a

trained smile, pronouncing her name like the country. 'Welcome to Kenya.'

* * *

The topography was familiar to her: the knuckle of the Ngong Hills, the Athi Plains, the towers of downtown Nairobi. Nothing had changed in two decades. It had just become more of what it was becoming when she left, more of what it was everywhere else. She knew Nairobi the way she knew Palm Springs, if she ever went back there, or Tahoe, the Black Hills, the Ruby Mountains. This was one of the reasons she never went back, she didn't wish to witness the slow murder of beauty, the greed and the self-righteousness of the murderers. One day the whole planet would be vacant lots, empty beer cans and chain link fences.

Ellie passed the tyre factory on the city's outskirts, the warehouses and car parts stores, new names but the same locations. She knew the roads and where they led, Langata, the train station, the industrial area, Mombasa. The knowledge was almost cellular, a map imprinted on her brain, like a migratory bird. She would always be able to find her way along these roads laid down by her race.

It was dry this year, the rains long past due.

47

The city seemed skeletal, leached of vitality. Plastic bags flapped on barbed wire fences like demented birds. Roadkill dogs decayed where they fell. People waited for their buses, coughing from diesel fumes, their shoes scuffed with red dust. The women held their handbags close and the men wore ill-fitting suits and clutched cheap briefcases. And on the barren verges, Maasai grazed their skinny cattle.

Her driver gestured to them. 'Maasai,' he said with a tour-guide's assurance. 'They come here wanting grass for their cows but there is nothing. You can see. They will not let you take a picture.' As if she'd want to. The Maasai lingered in their filthy shukkas. Most of them were boys, thin as saplings, dark as shadows, not the proud warriors with spears and beads the tourists came to see.

'But you can go to Bomas of Kenya,' the driver continued, determined to be helpful. 'There are Maasai dancers, also Kikuyu dancers and I think some Giriyama from the coast. You can ask for me to take you. My name is Eric.'

'Thank you, Eric,' she said. 'I'll keep that in mind.'

At a traffic light, street boys crowded around the car. They kept their bottles of glue in the sleeves of their ragged shirts. They had only pieces, buttonholes. If you put all their clothing together, you might fashion one complete shirt. One boy wore a single shoe, the others were barefoot.

Eric pressed the autolock. He was embarrassed by the boys, believing the cities of the West were without such human refuse. Ellie thought of when she'd lived in LA and the boy prostitutes she'd pass every night on her way home. They'd joke and jive her so she'd know how tough they were. But from month to month she never saw the same faces, always new boys with brave words and bad skin, and she could never bring herself to ask where the old ones had gone.

The glue boys pressed up against the taxi's windows, their filthy hands smudging the glass. There was no desperation or accusation in their eyes: they were beyond that. They were feral, they crawled through the sewers and ate out of garbage cans, and at the end of it, they limped onto the roundabouts and died in the bougainvillea bushes or up against the seams of buildings. The city scooped them into garbage bags with the rest of the litter and took them out to the dump. They were no heavier than paper and were without density, as ghosts.

The light changed and the boys were gone, dancing jauntily through the moving cars,

49

princes of poverty. Another half mile and Eric turned off the highway into an oasis of palm trees and Mercedes.

'Welcome, Madame!' The doorman snapped to attention, brass buttons, epaulettes, white gloves. The hotel hadn't been here before, Ellie remembered, just trees and old women selling charcoal. The adjacent highway ran up to Hurlingham, where there had been a bakery and hot buns in wax paper after school.

Inside the hotel, the lobby gleamed. Flowers arced out of huge brass vases: birds of paradise, tiger lilies. Businessmen gathered in reams of tropical-weight wool, the tourists in a herd of freshly pressed khaki. Someone brought her a juice on a tray, someone else gave her an orchid. She was shown to her room, past the glass cabinets displaying artefacts of the Turkana and Samburu tribes in the wild north — delicate leatherwork, beads the colour of dust or sky: a wedding gift, a ceremonial necklace, a symbol of womanhood. And in the elevator, more of the fantasy Africa was offered: a swimming pool in the Serengeti, a balloon ride at dawn, giraffe at sunset.

It was a gimmick, she thought, a Potemkin village. In America, this was how Africa had come to her, as one long wildlife documentary or adventure — or as the latest disaster news story; famine, war, floods, drought. She hadn't recognized it, it had been someone else's Africa, not Rosa's Africa. Not Baptist's Africa. Not music and sweet tea behind the kitchen.

Ellie's room overlooked Uhuru Park, which had been created in the early sixties to commemorate the freedom fighters who brought independence to Kenya. Now it seemed little more than a campground for the country's losers: the homeless AIDS victims, the glue boys, the unemployed, the happy clappers who praised their merciful, all-powerful Lord with megaphones and day long sing-a-longs.

But night fell and the city vanished, cleansed of its sins by the dark. Beyond the park, the city lights sparkled and below, on the patio around the turquoise swimming pool, guests laughed and drank cold beer.

Ellie lay on the vast bed, switched on CNN and ordered room service. When her food came she tipped the waiter outrageously because all she could think about was dusty shoes at bus stops, weary women clutching their handbags. She flipped the channels, old movies, bad movies, sitcoms.

Idly, she picked up the phone book and found the listing: 'Cameron, J. Mr' She dialled the number. Six months ago he would have answered. What would she have said? Now it rang and rang and disconnected.

Who buried him?

Surely there must have been one friend who buried him. Or burned him.

5

Sometimes Uncle Stanley took Helen with him as he went on his rounds. The estate covered ten square miles. About ninety percent of that was sugar; the staff housing, staff schools, hospital, cemetery, the main house and gardens, guest quarters, refinery, offices and individual staff plots took up the rest. There was even a small film theatre which showed out-of-date news pictorials and even older films for free on Saturday nights. The place was always packed.

Gesturing to all this, Stanley said (almost the same little speech, word for word, each time, like a mantra), 'I take good care of my watu. You've got to ask what independence will do for them. Nothing. They don't care about votes, they care about having a roof over their heads, food in their bellies, vaccinations for their children.' Stanley had strict rules about healthcare: all children were vaccinated for measles, smallpox and polio.

It was hot and humid in the cane fields. The workers wrapped their shirts around their heads. Their black bodies were shiny with sweat. Helen thought of racehorses, gleaming black muscle, all that power restrained by a scrap of leather the width of a rein.

Uncle Stanley liked to watch them. He liked the sound of the heavy machetes slashing the thick, green cane and the smell of the cane sap. Sometimes, the workers would sing, low and soft in their own language. But they would stop when the Bwana's Land Rover approached. They would briefly acknowledge the car, turning their eyes in its direction. Whatever they thought about their mzungu boss and their own endless days of sweat was buried deep in their skulls, unmineable.

Of course they didn't think very much according to Uncle Stanley. He said life was simple for them and death didn't mean the same thing because it happened all the time, like lunch or Sunday. They worked, they took a wife, had too many children — most of whom died. They got drunk, worked some more. They never thought ahead. It was just one day to the next with them. Any idiot knew you couldn't feed more than four children on a cane cutter's salary, but they kept on having them. Exponentially. The problem, as Uncle Stanley saw it, was that the black man had no ambition. While the white man was constantly moving forward, bettering himself and society, the black man was off drinking pombe in the shade or getting his wife pregnant. Or his wife's sister. 'They're lucky to have us,' he said. 'They'll see that when they get their blasted Independence. Without the whites, the whole bloody place'll fall apart at the seams. They'll be begging us to come back.'

In two years, Kenya was slated for nationhood, Uganda in a few months. Tanzania was already independent. The Italians had given up Somalia and Ethiopia. The Belgians had surrendered Burundi, Rwanda, Zaire. All through the continent, Africans were chanting 'Uhuru! Uhuru!' Except down south. Aunt B had confessed to Helen that she had written letters to her cousin in Rhodesia asking him about farming possibilities down there. She didn't want Stanley to know. It would break his heart to leave this place. But Aunt B was less attached to the land and therefore less romantic about it. One farm was as good as another. And in Rhodesia they'd never let the bloody Africans get the upper hand. It would always be white.

This distinction between black and white made Helen uncomfortable. There were so few blacks in England that she'd never had to think about it. But here there was no escaping the blackness of their skin, the whiteness of hers, the separateness of the two worlds. White and black lives only intersected where money was involved, and then without pleasure or friendship or respect. She didn't like the way Aunt B treated her servants — she yelled a lot, was abusive and insulting. She suspected that Stanley's brand of paternalism was really just racism.

Still, the Africans seemed to accept such behaviour towards them, even expect it, and it was true: they were slow to learn, not particularly interested in work, prone to forgetting and breaking things.

And anyway, who was Helen to judge anything? She knew herself incapable of properly thinking through such complexities as race relations and politics. She wanted to think only about the good things here, like the smiling children on the roadside and her friends at the club. She was just a pretty young woman enjoying her life.

★   ★   ★

On the eve of Uganda's Independence, October 9, 1962, they were driving home from the club in Jinja, Stanley at the wheel. There had been a party, a band and dancing. Everyone had drunk too much. Aunt B was asleep in the front seat. Helen, in the back, watched the road over Stanley's shoulder, a narrow corridor of light slicing through total darkness.

Stanley was drunk but he could still drive well enough. He could see some Africans on the road ahead waving him down. He didn't want to stop but he saw that a tree had fallen across the road. If he'd been sober, he might not have stopped. He might have thrown the car into reverse and driven back to the club. Sober, he might have known better.

He stopped. Bloody stupid Africans. Want to run their own country but can't move a bloody tree by themselves.

Something banged against the bonnet, the roof, his door, and then he, B and Helen were awake, sober in an instant. All Helen could make out in the darkness was the flash of a white shirt. Stanley tried to back up, but they were behind the car now, all around it. Hands rattled the doors and thumped against the car. Men were out there, skins the colour of night.

Hands, faces, white teeth, machetes. They were rocking the car. They smashed the back window. Arms reached in, tentacles blindly grabbing. Helen could not move or speak. Aunt B was screaming, Stanley was shouting: 'GET OFF! GET OFF THE FUCKING CAR!'

A face against the window: white eyes streaked with red. They began to chant 'Mzungu! Mzungu!' and the car tipped up on its side.

Stanley slammed his hand on the horn and held it there. The horn blasted into the night. The men smashed another window. There were hands in Helen's hair, smearing across her face, and the acrid smell of old sweat. And then they had Stanley's door open and they dragged him out.

Aunt B screamed, their black hands on her white legs, pulling her into the dark maw of night, and Helen clawing, hitting blindly.

And then suddenly it stopped.

The hands lifted, vanished. There was shouting, running, lights. The sound of a shot, then nothing, silence, cicadas.

Aunt B was moaning.

'Are you all right?'

A man's voice.

'Jesus God,' he said.

Helen saw his face as he leaned into the car, his blue eyes filled with concern. And she knew. She knew why all of this had happened, why she was here, why he was here, why time and space had tilted to these exact co-ordinates.

His name, she would find out, was John Cameron.

She married him four months later.

6

The sun shone through a break in the curtains, but it carried no fragrance or bird song or traffic sound. For a moment Ellie forgot where she was and she held her breath. Then, from down the hall, came the moan of a vacuum cleaner. She heard voices from the pool, car horns, the clinking of glassware, and exhaled.

Beside her remained a vast expanse of untrammelled white sheet, and she thought involuntarily of Peter and how he would have understood the moment he walked through the door of his house, before he even said, 'Hey, sweetie' from the hallway and she hadn't answered. He would have taken a beer from the fridge and sat down at the kitchen table. He would have expected it. He might even remember that she'd explained it all, earlier in the winter.

Earlier in the winter when he had taken her to Bosque del Apache where the snow geese gathered on the marshes.

Peter drove with his arm around the back of the Suburban's big bench seat, not holding her but encompassing her. They travelled down from Santa Fe, through the wastelands of outer Albuquerque, the casinos and the car dealerships, the interstate directed by the steep rise of the Sandia mountains to the east and the slow, brown swathe of the Rio Grande to the west. Winter had stripped the landscape bare, thrown out the brash furnishings of autumn, all that gaudy gold.

Ellie loved the winters. They were linear and clean. She could see the structure of things, the hinges and beams of trees and buildings, of housing estates and intersections, where canyons cut mountains, where narrow paths dodged among aspen groves. Sound moved differently in winter, unmuted and sharp as an arrow. She could hear an axe hewing through wood a mile away. In the evenings, the cattle from Santa Fe's outlying ranches gathered homeward, their lowing full of yearning for hay and warmth.

Never having had winter as a child, snow and ice were strange and wonderful to her. Snow changed everything, a blizzard was its own season. She even loved the shabby days that followed, how the snow decayed on sidewalks or shrivelled and hardened in the shadows. In the piñon forest behind their house, Peter had taught her how to read animal spoor in the snow. Here, a raven's wing, and here, last night, a coyote passing through.

They pulled into the Big Indian Motel. What remained of last week's snow had stubbornly fixed itself in place, a glossy white icing that flashed in the winter sun. The receptionist showed them to their room, which was decorated with a bird motif. There were ducks on the curtains and the bedspread was the colour of algae. Ellie thought it was very funny. She showed Peter the wallpaper in the bathroom, with flocks of ducks rising from three blue brushstrokes of water, but the paper was hung incorrectly and so the ducks were on a collision course.

The next morning, before dawn, they crept out into the stellar cold, their boots cracking the old snow, the night still tucked in firmly behind the hills. They drove out to the refuge. Already, there was a line of cars alongside the marshes, mostly old people, bundled up, sipping coffee, peering through binoculars. Peter and Ellie sat on the hood of the big Suburban with a thermos of coffee. Peter drew her close to keep her warm and she curled into him.

The snow geese clotted the water's dark surface, still and tightly folded as origami. Then light broke in the southeast, gold rimmed the low, black hills, and the birds began to stutter awake. Within minutes, they gathered themselves, squawking and fluttering, and rose up in one swoop. They lifted and wheeled and flung themselves against the silver air. Peter and Ellie watched like children.

When they got back to the motel, they made love on the pea-green bed. He held the lean chassis of her body. How perfectly her hipbones fitted his hands. Her hair was loose, tumbling, and she said his name with her breath against his neck. He wanted to open her up, he wanted to find the seams of her, some way in. He wanted to know the secrets she stored, all that she held back from the world, all that she hoarded from him.

'Why won't you let me in?' he said afterwards with his head on her belly and his hands on her ribcage, 'These are ribs not prison bars.'

'There's nothing in there,' she said and laughed softly, her fingers in his hair.

He looked up at her, his chin in his hand. 'I don't know anything about you.'

'That's not true,' her eyes slipped away from his and he knew the rest of her would follow, like mercury, so he held her, turned her face back to his. She said, 'You know I like dark chocolate and hot baths, thrillers and truck-stop coffee. You know my birthday, my middle name.'

'Ellie, it's a weapon for you, what you don't tell me, something to use against me.'

She lay back as if relaxing, but he could feel the tension in her body, her toes clenching. She thought she could lie to him but he was learning.

'What do you want?' she said.

'Tell me one thing about you, one thing you don't want to talk about.'

Still she wouldn't look at him and he could feel her leaving her body. He held her hands. She said, 'There isn't anything, just what we all have, memories, experiences, dreams, some good, some bad. It's not like there's some key you're going to find and suddenly you can fix me, or whatever it is you want. You think I know you because I know pieces of your past or that you like Miles Davis? You hate films with subtitles, whatever. We can become familiar to each other but we still can't get past our skin. The boundary is always there, don't you see?'

He let her move away from him, watched her walk across the room.

'What we share of ourselves — it's all we have,' he said. 'I'm not seeking some grand communion, just — '

Just what? He tried to think of the word or

words, the noun, the verb. He thought of how wood fitted together, how you built a table or a house. 'Just some kind of connection,' he said.

She was in the bathroom with the taps running, but she heard him. He was almost angry: 'I love you.'

What we share of ourselves, it's all we have.

But it isn't enough, she had thought. It isn't anything.

★ ★ ★

The taxi drove through Nairobi where the ghosts of old buildings loitered between new ones. It was as if she was seeing the streets, mosques and markets in the half-light of a deepest dusk; as if, squinting, the template of the past might align with that of the present. The names of the streets she recalled like childhood friends of whom she might ask, 'Whatever happened to him?' Opposite the market, she saw Bazaar Street, where thirty years ago Indian merchants owned shops of sequins and diamond buttons and silks. On the pavement had been beggars who terrified her.

That narrow lane with shops full of objects of desire, ribbons, coloured reams of cloth, gleaming boxes under dusty counters — once she had coveted a silver and gold bird ornament, all that pleasure and lust had been paid for with fear. To touch emerald satins and velvet brocade, she had had to submit to the touch of the beggars. Their fingers on the hem of her skirt, their fingers rough with the dread of their need. She had always thought it was called Bizarre Street.

Now, the street was like every other street. Groups of men stood in front of shabby storefronts, or they leaned against cars, pillars, trees. They sat on steps and watched cars drive by, or watched nothing at all. Slack-eyed, they waited for opportunities that didn't exist, for small jobs, delivering messages, sweeping offices, a few shillings even, that might buy food, a cigarette, a bottle of Coke.

These men stood outside the tall building where the taxi stopped. They looked briefly at Ellie as she walked past, and she was aware of the instinct with which she suddenly held her handbag tighter. In the cool, marble lobby the security guard was demanding IDs, but he didn't ask her. Because she was white. Her skin and her laundered shirt absolved her.

She took an elevator to the tenth floor. The offices were smart and neat, wood-panelled, as you'd expect. Mr Boudreau's secretary said he would be with her shortly and offered her tea or coffee. Ellie sat on the sofa and flipped through a wildlife magazine. The pages were full of trouble: overgrazing, poaching, corruption. The animals and the wild places were dying, the forests were sacrificed for charcoal, and a Canadian mining consortium was trying to build an opencast titanium mine near a coastal reserve. The same people got richer and the same people got screwed.

Mr Boudreau opened his door and held out his hand. He was a tall slim man, white-haired, immaculate in his appearance. 'Ms Cameron, I'm Richard Boudreau. Please come in.'

Dickie B, she thought. What was he to my mother?

★   ★   ★

They went into his office. Bookshelves of leather-bound law books centred around a large oak desk, the view from the windows was out over the city.

'How was your trip?' He gestured to two leather armchairs.

'Long,' she said. 'But the hotel is very nice. Thank you for arranging it.'

'And this is the first time you've been back since you left, in 1976?'

66

'Yes,' she said.

'You must notice a great deal of change.'

'I'm not sure what I remember, so I can't tell what's changed.'

'Everyone tends to be very pessimistic. But it's not all bad.' Mr Boudreau smiled, lifted a folder from the low table between them. 'Would you like another tea?'

'I'm fine, thanks.'

He opened the folder. 'Your father left a substantial estate. Fortunately, he got most of it out of the country. There is a portfolio in the Channel Islands. Having sold the house ten years ago, he no longer had property here, but he retained several local bank accounts. From these, as per your father's instructions, we have paid outstanding debts, including staff wages. There was just his housegirl in the end. His car has been sold, and the few pieces of furniture of value were auctioned. However, there remains a box of personal effects which he asked be given to you. You are, of course, the sole inheritor of your father's estate.'

Ellie was staring at a print of an elephant on the wall. Your father, your father, your father. Words from a long time ago. 'Your father is very tired.' 'Your father isn't well.' 'Your father didn't mean it.' Your father — an excuse, a threat. And anyway, he wasn't hers, nor she his, genes did not grant ownership.

'I'd prefer it if we referred to him as John Cameron,' she said.

Mr Boudreau nodded politely, 'I understand.'

But did he? How could he? She looked at his manicured hands, French cuffs, silver cufflinks. He understood nothing about hiding in the dark, knowing the sound of your heart would give you away. Instead, he'd think she was a bitch, some neurotic feminist.

'It's just — ' she started, her hands in front of her, grappling.

'It's none of my business.' He nodded, a smile, practised but still reassuring.

She let her hands drop to her knees. 'What do I need to sign?'

He handed her the folder. 'Where I've indicated with the blue tabs. The date also, please.'

She signed.

He told her the accounts in Jersey would automatically be transferred into her name. Ellie saw the amount.

'He was good with money,' she said.

'Yes,' said Mr Boudreau. 'He was one of the best accountants this country ever had.'

'You knew him well?'

Mr Boudreau smiled kindly. 'For many

years. We played golf together. But not recently. I hadn't seen him for quite some time.'

'And this box?'

'I'll have my secretary get it for you.'

He rang through, spoke to his secretary. She appeared with a cardboard box that had once contained Chilean wine. Ellie glanced inside and saw what looked like the contents of a desk drawer: a debris of papers.

'What is this for?'

'He was very particular that it be given directly to you,' Mr Boudreau said.

'But why?' She noted the old magazines, the petrol receipts.

He turned his hands palms up. There was no explanation. He told her instead about the transactions to follow and how he'd send the remaining paperwork to her hotel. At the end of it he leaned back slightly, shutting the folder. 'If there's anything else, please give me a call.'

Ellie did not think there would be anything else. Her flight was in three days.

'Just enough time to take in the sights of Nairobi,' Mr Boudreau noted. 'Such as they are.'

★   ★   ★

That afternoon she lay by the pool with the other tourists: a honeymoon couple, a fat German woman with legs like cooked sausages, a few Americans who slathered themselves in sunblock and worried about the transmission of the Ebola virus and whether the ice was germ-free. Children were splashing and screaming in the water while an elderly Asian man gently swam laps, his head raised like a terrapin above the waterline. There was no sign of the drought here, the grass was thick and green, the gardens lush.

A sunbird hovered over the hibiscus, the same bird shown on the stamp, and the name now came to her: scarlet-chested. And in a rush came other names connected to the same spool of memory: bee-eater, roller, hamerkop, fire finch. And then Swahili words: mbwa, mauua, twiga, kibiriti, farasi, barabara, pole pole. With the words came images scatter-shot. *Barabara*. Red earth-road through green up-country fields, or the road home from school in the sleepy hot afternoon under the long shadows of gum trees, or the road along the edge of the Rift Valley where you could see God in the clouds. *Kibiriti*. Rosa lighting her jiko with kibiriti, her tea brewing thick and sweet in a blue enamel pot. *Mauua*. Flowers were everywhere, the tame roses in the garden and the bolts of colour in the long grass beyond the house. *Mvua*. Rain, which was elements and senses combined; it was cloud, grass, taste, smell. But mostly it was green, a mad, impossible green that hijacked the entire country for months at a time. Rain was the longing at the end of the dry season when everything was brittle and covered in dust, longing for the words spoken by Pious the shamba boy. Ellie would wait for him, looking up at his old mouth that folded in on itself because he had no teeth, longing for him to break the spell of the dust, and cast his own: 'Mvua itanyesha.' The rain is coming. Sometimes it would take days, the sound and smell of it like an advance party for the thunderclouds and fat drops that fell one, then two, puffing the dust, and then in a stampede that set free all the flowers and trees, butterflies and flying ants.

All these years Ellie had carried these memories with her. Not forgetting but resisting. All these years she had contained the language, her throat a vessel for the Arabic and the Bantu, a half-caste, magpie language concocted by travellers and traders as they traversed the palm-green shores and waded deep into the merciless beauty of the interior. *Lala salaama, maendeleo, mtoto yangu*. Rosa's language, the language of Baptist's radio: her native tongue.

She had found a path back, unexpectedly, accidentally, but still she hesitated to turn that way, to speak and to remember.

★ ★ ★

Later, when the shadows arched over the pool, Ellie went back to her room. She wanted to smoke, although she had not smoked in years. She opened the mini-bar instead and mixed a gin and tonic, that elixir of Empire Builders. Gin, in her experience, made you brave, which meant you lost your inhibitions and your conscience, virtues that needed to be discarded when you were building empires.

The box from her father squatted in the corner like some awful piece of garden statuary given by a well-meaning aunt. Unavoidable, awkward, karmically impossible to throw away. How fitting that his effects should be contained in something that once contained alcohol.

Even dead he was a drunk.

She didn't care — the gin had made sure of that — but she looked inside, rifled through the back issues of the *East African Wildlife Society* magazine, the news letters from his accounting firm, two decades old, the telephone receipts and old Christmas cards from business associates. Everything was at least ten years old, as if he had left his life in 1990, not two months ago.

Why had he wanted her to have this? She turned the box out onto the floor. Was there some clue she was supposed to find that might hint at a bid for absolution? An explanation? A confession? She sifted through. Not a photograph, not a letter, no trace of anything save a man who paid his bills on time. Is this what he wanted her to know? I was a shit for a father but I paid my bills on time.

She called Richard Boudreau.

He was just leaving his office but his secretary caught him at the door.

Ellie worried that she sounded drunk. Her voice was quavering, not quite her own. He might think like father, like daughter.

'When did my father die?'

'Are you all right?' His voice calm, measured. She imagined him standing with his briefcase.

'I'm not — I don't — ' She started again. 'I just have a few questions.'

'I'll do my best.'

'When did he die?'

'December 28.'

'Was he in hospital?'

'He was in his flat.'

73

'And where was that?'

Mr Boudreau hesitated — or perhaps he was just remembering. 'The Brunswick Apartments. Up the hill from the Pan Afric hotel.'

When she hung up she realized she had said 'my father'.

7

Helen had worn a pale blue dress and pillbox hat with a short veil to the ceremony. She had dreamed all her life of a white dress, silk with a tulle overlay, and small pink rosettes embroidered around the neck. But John had been married before, so white and the church were forbidden to her. Somehow she was less because he was. But that was marriage, wasn't it? Sharing everything, even mistakes.

Her parents hadn't come out, it was too far to fly. They'd met John in England shortly after their engagement, had appreciated his solvency, willingly blessed the marriage, and gone back to their bridge games and gardening. They'd sent flowers, a big bouquet of white carnations. In their stead, the Wickses had driven down from Uganda. Aunt B stood as Helen's witness at the registry office in Nairobi's City Hall, beaming and clucking as if she was responsible. Uncle Stanley stood apart from them, the only real guest, looking awkward in his suit and tie, his feet constricted in polished shoes.

After the ceremony, John had arranged a small reception at the Muthaiga Club for his partners from the firm, for B and Stanley, and Roy and Eileen McMullen who were John's neighbours in Kitisuru.

Aunt B threw rice and Stanley had tied old beer cans to the rear bumper of John's car. The guests said 'Good luck! Good luck!' 'All the best!' 'Drive safely!' The newly-weds drove to the airport with the cans clanking all the way, dripping with rice, and climbed into John's plane.

They flew up to the Aberdare Mountains. Helen was afraid of flying but she was determined not to be silly, some flighty young girl, but a woman who embraced her life. He was a good pilot and she didn't want him to think she didn't trust him. The mountains were beneath them, clear of mist in the afternoon, a rumpled, jungled green with the occasional knife flash of a waterfall in the deep canyons. Every bump in the flight sent her heart to her throat, but she stifled her cries and secretly wiped her sweaty palms on the rough cloth of her seat.

John had booked the honeymoon suit at the Aberdare Country Club, a rambling stone lodge on the edge of the forest. It was cold, the air translucent. She could see Mount Kenya rising in the distance, Africa all around her.

They checked in and John took her hand as

they walked to their room across the emerald lawn, past the tumbling flowerbeds and the aviary with bright, loud birds. She could tell he was nervous because he talked about irrelevant things, the weather, the bird life. John was not a talker. She'd tried, when they had first started seeing each other, to engage him, but found she was nattering away by herself and that what she was saying was utterly inane. John was simply content to have her with him, as he read his paper or smoked his pipe. And anyway, they did talk about important things: where to live, his work, Kenya's independence. She was certain that as their life together deepened they would have more to share, the way couples did, chattering about children, a possible addition to the house, their friends' marriages. This was only the beginning, she had to be patient. She didn't want to be one of those pushy, demanding women.

When they reached the door to their cottage, John picked her up and carried her over the threshold. They were both laughing, and Helen hoped her laughter sounded genuine, because, in fact, she felt awkward, unsure. She had no idea what to do when he put her down, so she kept laughing and playfully hit him with her bouquet. He grabbed her, with mock roughness, and kissed her. It was a real kiss, with his tongue, the way Charlie had once kissed her. French kissing, he had told her.

John pulled her close, kissing her harder, his fingers fumbling with the buttons on her dress. She knew she was supposed to be the heroine succumbing to her passion at last. She wanted to feel again what she had felt the first time he touched her, lifting her from Uncle Stanley's car: safe, but also fragile, profoundly feminine.

But now she wanted it to stop, for it to be okay for her to withdraw, for it to be enough for them to chat and play cards or perhaps go for a walk hand in hand. She made herself limp in his arms, as she imagined he expected, as if weak from desire.

At last he released her. 'You are so lovely,' he said. 'I can't wait any more.' He stepped back, and she understood the command. This is what women did. She was married now. She would be like those other wives she saw, arriving at cocktail parties with their husbands, linked by the intimacy of touch and look, sharing private jokes. She wasn't a girl any more but a wife.

She took a bath and changed into her nightdress, a long sheath of white satin with lace-scalloped edging. Something at least was white. Trembling, afraid of her own inexperience, she looked in the mirror and saw that what John said was true, she was lovely. Suddenly, she felt powerful, her beauty was her power, she was wanted, desired and therefore worthy. She remembered Simon Dennett's hand on the small of her back and understood now that his desire for her had funnelled from his whole body to his fingertips. Letting down her hair, Helen stepped into the bedroom.

It was over after a sharp pain and John contracting above her, then the wetness between her thighs that she immediately wanted to wash away. He rolled off her and beside her now, reached over with his hand and touched her face.

'It'll get better,' he said.

She could not even imagine what he meant. It seemed an act without potential for pleasure. She could not understand the stories of women seeking out affairs, ruining marriages, reputations, leaving their children for this. Perhaps she was frigid. She'd heard of such women. Frigid was an awful word, a combination of rigid and fridge, so she would be cold and hard, an object, a box, a utility.

But John's hand was on her face, and she looked into his eyes and saw kindness there. He loved her and she loved him and she was overwhelmed with tenderness. I want to take care of you, he'd said when he'd asked her to marry him. I want to make everything right for you, he said with his touch. Even this.

Soon, he fell asleep, leaving her alone. She watched him, thinking: my husband. She was sure there would be no worse, no poorer, no sickness, not for them in this precious circle of love that bound them. When he woke, he wanted her again. After that, she dressed for dinner, a deep blue silk dress that she'd had made by a tailor on Bazaar Street; it had cost her a fortune, the last of the money she'd made in Uganda. But what did money matter now?

$$\star \quad \star \quad \star$$

He drank that night, whisky, champagne, wine with dinner, then more whisky. After all, there was so much happiness to celebrate. Over dinner, she told him about her childhood, their house on the outskirts of the village, the donkeys across the street. She fed them carrots. They had soft noses and woke her father with their braying.

After dinner they withdrew to the lounge where a huge fire blazed in the stone fireplace. The night outside was so thick and dark it seemed to press against the windows like a black cat wanting in. The bushbabies screamed in the forest, their awful, bleeding-woman scream. But they were sweet, small, furry animals after all, a joke the Forest Djinn played on the uninitiated. Helen felt far away from anything and everyone she knew. Which was good, which was really just newness, the newness of her new life.

By the fire sat another couple John knew, a balding man with his plump young wife, farmers from Nanyuki, Quentin and Gilly Baruch. Gilly giggled too much and drank too much. Well, they all drank too much that night, but Gilly outpaced even John. Quentin did a lot of complaining: he was sick of the lazy Africans. Gilly carried on conversations that were nothing to do with his as if they were at separate tables.

'They let their cattle graze until there's no grass left, not a single bloody blade, and then they come running to me: 'Bwana, saidia, givee us more landee for our gombees, they are dyingee,' ' Quentin said, exaggerating a Kikuyu's heavily accented English in which the endings of words were drawn out. He made a motion as if he was picking his nose.

Gilly was saying, 'Everyone knows Errol was working for MI5 and they had him murdered. It was nothing to do with Diana, that fat tart, really, she's very plain, we saw her at the polo a few months ago. The whole love-triangle thing was something she put about just to give herself some glamour, because she doesn't have any of her own, and her hair is very badly dyed.'

Gilly and Quentin did so much talking that Helen and John didn't have to say a word. Which was a relief because Helen was tipsy, and she didn't want to talk anyway, she just wanted to sit there, lazy and hazy, looking at John and thinking: my husband, my husband. There was such magic in those words. Whatever happened in their bed was separate from this pride of place she felt with him. It would get better. She rubbed the ring on her finger with her thumb, feeling it there, knowing that everyone who met her would see this ring and know that she belonged to John Cameron.

At what point did she become aware that John was watching the farmer's wife? Or think he was, because it might have been something she created in her mind, for she had no experience of jealousy and none of alcohol. Then she became sure of it. John was looking at Gilly and she was sitting with her legs curled beneath her, her knees pointing at him. Gilly's eyes were cat eyes, unblinking and unashamed.

Helen did not want to be there anymore. She felt sick from the drink and she wanted to be alone with John so he could tell her he loved her, so he could kiss her with tender kisses and hold her in his strong arms, so she could know she had been wrong. She yawned, hoping he would see her. But instead he ordered another round of drinks. She shifted in her seat, so the blue silk dress rode slightly up her thighs. Perhaps if he desired her, he would want to go back to their room.

But Gilly was giggling and saying: 'Oh my, it's very dangerous when I get so tipsy!'

'And why is that?' John asked her. Helen was watching them. Gilly's voice and John's voice seemed preternaturally loud, as if they were shouting to each other. And Helen, watching Gilly's cat eyes, watching his eyes. Even the watching was loud.

Gilly said, 'I get myself into all kinds of trouble!'

Quentin was sitting back in his chair, his eyes half-closed.

'What kinds of trouble?' John said.

Helen tried to reason with herself: John was just talking with this woman, just asking her a question. It was all in fun, a grown-up game. He was flirting with her, so what? That didn't mean he would have it off with her.

Quentin let out a bark of a laugh. He spoke without moving from deep in his chair, his eyes still half-closed. 'She fucks when she gets drunk. She fucks. She fucks the cook, she fucks the shamba boy, she fucks dogs. But only black dogs, mind.' He looked at Helen. 'No need to worry, she won't fuck your husband. Wrong colour.'

In an instant, Gilly's eyes hardened. The soft, pouty lips retracted into a line. 'Shut up, damn you,' she said.

For an absurd moment, Helen imagined Aunt B saying at such a juncture, 'Shall we move into the drawing room for coffee?'

'You horny bitch,' Quentin said, without malice, without care.

Gilly threw her drink at him, but missed, the glass shattering on the floor. 'I hate you!' she said, her features twisting and flocking toward the centre of her face in a snarl. 'I fucking hate you! The sight of you makes me sick.'

'Be sick then.' Quentin took a sip from his drink.

Helen put her hand on John's wrist. She wanted to go. She wanted to run from this. She didn't want to know this was possible.

Gilly got up and walked slowly from the room. She reached the door. 'It's only because you can't get it up, you pathetic little shit.' And she went out into the night.

'Another round?' Quentin said, raising his hand to the waiter, who looked as if he'd seen nothing, sweeping the broken glass up off the floor.

'Please,' Helen said quietly to John. 'Please can we go?'

8

The next day Ellie took a taxi up Uhuru Highway and past the glue boys, the Maasai with their dying cattle on the roundabouts, past the drought-stricken jacarandas. The Brunswick Apartments had once been respectable, the kind of place, thirty years ago, that young English girls who were secretaries and receptionists lived in until they married and moved to big houses in white suburbs like Kitisuru or Karen or Kileleshwa. But now half-naked African children chased chickens around the overgrown parking lot. Windows were broken. There were plastic bags instead of blossoms on the bougainvillea bushes. There was a goat tied to a tree. Above everything hovered a haze of exhaust fume from the highway.

'Who are you looking for?' The taxi driver turned, leaning over the seat, looking at her. It was Eric, but he didn't remember her. She was just another tourist or aid worker, another mzungu.

'The manager,' she said.

'Wait. I go and look,' Eric said. He got out and walked into the main stairwell.

86

He came back with a fat woman in a T-shirt, kanga and flip-flops. Her stiff hair rose in a lopsided peak on the top of her head.

'Hello,' said Ellie. 'I'm sorry to bother you.'

The woman looked blank, made no reply.

'An old man, a mzungu, used to live here. He died just after Christmas.'

The woman stuck her finger in her ear and jiggled it violently. She then removed her finger and looked at the tip. Ellie turned to the driver, 'She doesn't speak English.'

'Mimi najua,' the woman said.

'She speaks,' Eric said.

Ellie looked again at the woman: 'Did you know him, the mzungu?'

'I knew him,' she said. 'But they took all his things away. There is nothing of his here.'

'I know. I just wondered which apartment was his.'

The woman sighed and shook her head. And then she burst into a long, angry diatribe in Swahili. Ellie could catch only words, the flow of the language eluded her. When the woman was done, Eric spoke back to her in Swahili. They spoke back and forth.

Eric shook his head. He looked disgusted. 'She wants money,' he said.

'For what?'

'She cannot rent the room.'

'Why not?'

'Because this mzungu, he is dying there.'

'But why does that matter?' Perhaps the neighbours warned prospective tenants. Perhaps there was superstition about a place of death.

The woman erupted again in Swahili.

Eric shook his head again. 'She is very rude, this woman, very rude.'

'What did she say?'

'She says the smell.'

'What smell?'

'The mzungu, he died and left a smell.'

'I don't understand,' Ellie said.

The woman made a tsss sound with her tongue and her teeth. 'He was died many days before he was taken away. Now his room smell.' She wrinkled her nose.

'Which apartment?'

She gestured to the third window along, the first floor.

'I want to see it,' Ellie said. 'Do you have a key?'

The woman didn't move.

'I'll pay you whatever you want,' Ellie said.

Reluctant still, the woman turned. Ellie followed her into the building. The hallway stank of urine. The woman dragged her flip-flops along the floor in a heartless shuffle. She stopped, removed a circle of keys from the folds of her kanga and opened a door. She stood beside it, making a show of her refusal to enter.

Ellie went in. Two rooms, a bathroom and a kitchen. Peeling paint, water stains on the ceiling and floor, the linoleum crumbling like stale bread. A half-dozen bluebottle flies hurled themselves at the window. Had they eaten his flesh? Of course not. Flies did not live so long.

It took some time for her to find the smell, for it was low-grade, hiding behind cleaning solvent. He had smelt of whisky and aftershave and now he smelt of this, of rotten meat.

She ran out, gagging.

★ ★ ★

At the hotel she made an inventory of the box:
- Ten copies of *Swara* magazine, vols. 21–31, 1986–1989
- telephone receipts from March 1985 to January 1990 (note: no overseas calls, no long distance)
- 33 Christmas cards from various unknown people, year of receipt unknown
- bill of Sale, September 14, 1989 for an

Audi Quattro @ Kshs 300,000/=
- one copy of book *Birds of Kenya*
- two *Playboys*, August 1985, November 1987
- brochure for Governor's Camp — safari lodge in Mara
- an empty address book — looks like bank freebie
- instruction booklet for toaster
- one silver (?) buffalo-head cufflink
- box of paperclips
- 1988 whole year's issues of the *Economist*
- restaurant receipt from Hilton Hotel June 16, 1989
- Cameron & Best newsletters 1979–1990

This was all.

In the folder Richard Boudreau had messengered over she found the receipt from Bishandas's Auction House for a small amount of furniture: a bed, several chairs, a table. Of his other possessions — clothing, bedding, pots, pans, shaving brush, tooth-brush, teacups — there was no record. Perhaps the neighbours had taken them. Perhaps there had been other things he wanted her to have but they had been pilfered. Only the box, containing nothing of value, remained.

She called Richard Boudreau. His secretary put her on hold. She waited. Finally, he came on the line.

'I'm sorry to bother you again,' she said.

'Please, don't be,' he said.

'What happened to everything else?'

There was a silence.

And then he said, 'You went to Brunswick.'

'Yes.'

'Look,' he said. 'What about lunch? The Norfolk Hotel. We can discuss things then. Just tell the taxi driver, 'Norfolk.' But maybe you remember it.'

★ ★ ★

The Norfolk was indeed as she remembered it, although it had burnt to the ground in the meantime. The owners had rebuilt it brick by brick, a homage to the colonial days. The open veranda, with its cobblestone floor and dark-timbered tables, was predictably crowded with tourists. Ellie wondered if the country they found in any way resembled their *Out of Africa* dreams. The poverty must have surprised and appalled them. But maybe they didn't see it, wilfully sticking to the script of campfires and cocktails.

Richard Boudreau wore an immaculate grey suit. The waiter knew him as a man of importance and presented the menus with an especially elaborate flourish.

'Still no rain,' he said as he sat with her. The sky was neither cloudy nor sunny, a barren canvas. 'The fish curry is very good.'

They ordered.

'It's funny,' he said, 'I remember when your — when John told me he was getting married again. My wife and I thought, 'Thank goodness.' His first wife — Jean, that was her name. She was a bit wild. 'Fast' as we said in my day. It ended badly. But then most marriages when they end, end badly.'

'Many marriages stay badly,' said Ellie.

He laughed gently. Though he must have been in his seventies, his skin was smooth and translucent, his thick, silver hair sleek and polished. She wondered if his wife was one of those memsahibs Julius Mwangi loathed, a starchy-haired blonde with a voice like a sharp poker. Lete gin and tonic haraka. Bring the gin and tonic quickly.

'We were very sad when the divorce happened again, when your mother left.'

Ellie studied the menu. 'I don't remember much about it.'

'But it must have been difficult. Leaving here, leaving him.'

'I didn't miss him and he never made an effort. We weren't close even before. I find it

peculiar that he should leave his money to
me.'

'You were — are — his daughter.'

'A cat's home, a distant cousin, I don't
know.'

'John had no one else,' he said. 'In the end.'

'How long was he dead before he was
found?'

'Four days. It was over Christmas, so many
people were away, visiting their relatives up
country. Or just busy. Family, work, the usual
sort of thing. It was the night watchman who
finally realized something was wrong. And
even then no one knew whom to call. A dead
mzungu brings complications. An African
always has a family. But to whom did this old
man belong? Who would pay for the
mortuary? He'd been living there for ten
years and he'd never had a visitor. The police
tracked down his housegirl. Her former
employers had known him. They had moved
back to England, but the firm they'd worked
for knew — and so on, until they found me.
I'd always been his lawyer. And more. Once,
his friend. He's buried out in Kiambu, a little
church there in the middle of a coffee farm. I
thought that's what he would want. His father
is buried there as well.'

His father, John's father. A stranger, dead a
decade before Ellie's birth, unremembered.

Not my grandfather, just His Father. There had been no affectionate anecdotes, no photographs, no flowers on the grave. Ellie imagined father and son, side by side, saying nothing to each other, forever.

'But why was he living there, such a wretched place? He had all that money.'

Richard sat back a moment. 'I don't know.'

'Maybe he just wanted to be left alone to drink?' she phrased it like a question, but it wasn't. It was what she believed.

He looked at her, but there was no rebuke in his expression. 'The last time I saw him was at the Aeroclub — you know, the bar out at the local airport. That was in 1992. We talked very briefly. He had retired a few years earlier and we didn't have much to say to each other. Before, we'd always had business gossip to keep us going. I invited him to call me, to make a date for lunch. I knew he wouldn't, and I suppose I felt a bit relieved. The loss of a friendship that has passed its prime never feels like a loss. I thought that he might be lonely. But that's all I thought. I'm a selfish man and I have a busy life. When I found out about his death, and the manner of it, I wanted to feel sad, because it is sad, a man reduced like that. Or at least guilty that I hadn't done more.'

Richard Boudreau paused and nodded to

an Asian man at a nearby table whom he recognized. 'But I was angry. All I could think was how much life had been wasted on him.'

He smiled, that practised lawyer's smile, but for himself this time.

'You see, I lost my daughter when she was twenty-one in a car crash on the Mombasa Road. And all I could think — still think — is why couldn't she have had the ten years, the twenty years that he didn't want?'

He touched his napkin to his mouth. 'I'm seventy-three and it still galls me how unfair life is.'

After a moment, Ellie said softly, 'I'm sorry.'

He looked at her. 'I don't know if I've told you anything helpful. Maybe I've been too personal.'

'I'm not sure what I'm after. Or why I came back. I shouldn't have. But I suppose it's just curiosity, to know how something ended. Even in a bad film we want to know what happens.'

'As I said, he was once a friend. I liked him. And he was respected.'

'Do you remember Eileen McMullen?' she said in a rush, not expecting herself to say it.

'Eileen. Yes. She killed herself. It was all very sad that. Poor Roy.'

Ellie remembered her mother explaining

the word 'suicide'. Mrs McMullen had killed herself, she was a sad, unhappy woman, poor thing.

'Thank you for your time — for everything.' Ellie made sure to smile and keep her voice even, her liar's voice. As he reached for the bill, she put her hand over it first. 'Please, let me. I have to spend that money somehow.'

He gently slipped his hand over hers. 'But I'm an old man and I seldom have lunch with a pretty young woman. It is entirely against my principles to let you pay.'

So she let him pay.

'And how is your mother?'

'She's fine, very happy.'

'Good,' he said as if he meant it. He left a generous tip. 'I'm glad it worked out. Will you tell her that?'

They walked together to the hotel's entrance. She turned to him: 'I must reimburse you for the cost of his burial, for whatever else.'

He touched her arm lightly. 'Please, Eleanor, I wanted to do it. I do not consider it a debt.' He hailed her a taxi.

But as her taxi pulled away, merging into the traffic, it occurred to her that perhaps Richard Boudreau knew all about how Eileen McMullen had really died. He had been her father's lawyer, a friend, they'd patted each other on the back out on the eighteenth green. He knew about the money in the Channel Islands, illegally taken out of the country. Why wouldn't he also know about Mrs McMullen?

⋆　⋆　⋆

Ellie gave the driver directions, not to the hotel, but to the house where she had once lived, far out in Kitisuru on the edge of the coffee farms. The coffee was gone; big new houses for UN staffers and ex-pats choked the hillsides. They turned left, uphill. Where once a few women hawked tomatoes and mealies on the corner, now there were stalls selling purple velvet sofas and varnished bookcases.

They drove on, under the arch of jacarandas and eucalyptus and she could see the sun glinting through the tall trees. She felt sleepy, as she once had sitting in the back of her mother's car on the black vinyl seat and watching the sky and the glinting trees though the window. This was where the road swooped down, then up and right. Here her mother would begin to slow down, she'd indicate, tick-tick and hoot the horn. The gates would creak open, Pious in his red knit hat and black gumboots, the hat worn even in the hot, dry season. The car turned right onto the long dirt driveway with the stripe of grass up the middle and the drooping bottle-brush trees and the barking dogs.

Here, here was my house. Once.

Now there was a mini-mall. A grocery, a pizzeria, an internet bureau, a hairdresser's, a video rental outlet.

Ellie got out of the taxi. She bought a Fanta for herself and one for the driver. He offered her a cigarette, a Sportsman, and she took it. Sitting on the hood of the car, she looked at the single-story cinderblock mini-mall. There is no python at the bottom of the garden anymore, like the one that ate our Siamese cat and the McMullens' dog, she thought, no wild things rustling and flickering in the long grass and the lileshwa groves that went for miles.

The house was gone, and she was suddenly glad. With all its unhappiness, its dark corners, the cupboards filled with fear. But she grieved for the garden, the lawn that fell away to bush, her sandpit and the tall, weeping pepper tree. In the garden she had been a child; skinny, brown, barefoot, solitary. Hours and hours of happiness, the smell and taste of certain leaves, black earth in her hands after the rain, the prick of the euphorbia tree and the trail of salty blood on her leg. She grieved for all the brown snakes and fire finches, the hawks and the lizards.

But the McMullens' house remained on the adjacent lot, whitewashed with a red-tiled roof, a certain Spanish flair, sealed from the road by the same cray-apple hedge and black iron gate. Sometime after Mrs McMullen had died, and after Ellie and her mother had left, Dr McMullen had also gone. He had taken the 'McMullen' sign with him.

And Baptist and Rosa? Where had they gone? Had they found jobs? Good jobs, people who paid them well, treated them well? Ellie finished the cigarette. She didn't want to think about them. Loving them still, decades on, she felt she was losing them still.

9

Baptist says: 'Kuja.' Come. Rosa is with him.

You follow them across the lawn from your house, through the gap in the hedge. You enter the McMullens' white house with the polished wood floor like glass. Baptist sometimes wears pads of sheepskin on his bare feet to shine these floors, shuffling the length of the corridor. Now, he is barefoot and the three of you move like thieves through the quiet afternoon of the house. Past Nina's room, empty without Nina now. Upstairs where you have never been, across the thick, red carpet on the landing.

Baptist leads you and Rosa into the McMullens' bedroom with the bed unmade, the pink bedcover thrown back, the white sheets, and here is the smell of Mrs McMullen, her face-powder and perfume. You see the dressing table with magic potions, glass bottles glimmering with amber liquid, a cool white pot of Pond's cold cream, a red lipstick with the silver cover off.

And a letter on paper decorated with roses under a glass paperweight.

You stop to touch these things but Rosa says 'Tssss.'

Baptist stands by the half-open bathroom door and will not enter. So you do, and see Mrs McMullen with the cord of her pink bathrobe around her neck. Mrs McMullen's eyes bulge and her mouth hangs open with her petal-pink tongue just visible. Her dressing gown has slipped apart. Her legs are lumpy and sprinkled with tiny purple veins.

'What happened?' You look up at Baptist.

Baptist has hands the size of toilet seats and he folds them away in front of him, hides them in his armpits. 'The bwana,' he says. 'Bwana Camera.'

Your father.

Rosa touches his arm.

'We have to call the police,' you say.

'Hapana!' Rosa says, frightened.

You look at Mrs McMullen. 'But the police will know what to do.'

Baptist stares down at his feet and shakes his head.

'They will say he did this,' says Rosa, looking at Baptist.

'But he didn't.'

Baptist looks at you fiercely. 'Bwana Camera was here. He did this. But they will say it was me because I am an African.'

He points to something in the wastepaper

basket but you don't know what it is, something dead, withered, or the skin of something.

Rosa says: 'He was here. Saa hii.' This time. 'Na halafu, alienda.' She makes a going away motion with her hands.

'Memsahib alipiga kelele sana,' says Baptist. Memsahib, she made a lot of noise.

'Ai ai ai.' Rosa shakes her head.

You look again at Mrs McMullen. You have never seen a dead person before. You reach out and touch her hand, the soft pale skin. Mrs McMullen does nothing. You think that you can kick her and she can do nothing about it. You stick out your tongue like Mrs McMullen.

Rosa grabs your shoulder, 'Toto!'

You retract your tongue. 'I hate her.'

Baptist is angry: 'What are you doing? You are playing when she is dead. The police, what will they do? This is not a time to play.'

You once heard a friend of your father's tell a story about an African who had been taken by the police: 'He's a cripple now. They broke his legs.' When the grown-ups saw you they said their code word, 'Paadayvonlayzonfon', and started talking about something else. But other times you sit on the stairs where they can't see you. 'Children should be seen and not heard,' they say.

Better if you are not heard and not seen either.

But you can still listen.

Will the police break Baptist's legs, which is what happens when dogs get hit by cars or horses fall in holes?

'We can tell the police the truth,' you say. They will arrest your father, take him away in the back of their car. Will they break his legs, too? You imagine him in a wheelchair, his legs covered in a tartan blanket. You will bring him hot chocolate and ginger biscuits, like Florence Nightingale. He will smile and say 'Thank you, my dearest child.'

Rosa says 'Tssss' again, and 'He is a mzungu. The police will say he cannot do this.'

You do not understand what you should do, what Rosa and Baptist expect you to do, only that because you are white this is your responsibility. You feel small and helpless and you begin to hate Mrs McMullen more because she has done this to you and Rosa and Baptist.

Then there is the sound of a car horn, your mum at the gate of your house, the dogs barking. Baptist covers his face with his hands and starts to moan. He sways back and forth moaning, sometimes making an 'Aaaaaa' sound. They will break his legs. Baptist will have no legs, he will be like the beggars on Bizarre Street dragging their twisted legs behind them, wearing flip-flops on their hands. The sound of breaking legs might be like a branch cracking.

You stand up and walk from the bathroom. As you walk through the bedroom you see the letter on the rose paper on Mrs McMullen's dressing table. You take it and put it in your shirt, without knowing why, only that the letter is something important, something powerful that you now have. You see Baptist take the paperweight and slip it in his pocket. Rosa takes the lipstick. These thefts bind you together, seal your secrecy.

Downstairs you run, and outside, through the hedge. Your mum is getting out of the car.

'Mum, Mum, Mum, Mrs McMullen's dead.'

Your mum's face suddenly strange.

'Baptist didn't do it. He didn't, Mum. He didn't do it.'

Your mum runs into the McMullens' house.

★ ★ ★

Later, the police come. The head policeman is a big fat mzungu with red hair. You are inside the house, not in your room where you

104

have been told to stay, but in the guest room where you can see over into the McMullens' driveway. Your mother is talking with the fat policeman. Baptist and Rosa are standing by the front door. Rosa is crying. Baptist is looking at the ground, his huge hands clasped in front of him.

The fat policeman takes him away. Rosa is screaming, trying to run after the car, and your mother is holding her back. You can see her saying, 'It's okay, it's okay,' but Rosa knows. She knows what the police do to house servants.

*   *   *

When Baptist comes back his legs are unbroken, but he is very quiet and unable to look up from the ground. He does not talk to you any more. He does not come to the shade behind the kitchen in the afternoons with his radio. Rosa says he is troubled, but the Lord will soon heal him. You wonder if he still has the paperweight, and perhaps Rosa still has the lipstick.

You have kept the letter, but you cannot read the grown-up writing, the words scrunched together with big loops like bad knitting. You keep it in your treasure box in the very back of your clothes cupboard. You crouch in there sometimes with the door closed and with a torch and try to read the letter. You hope that if you stare at it long enough you will be able to understand it, the way it would be nice if you would sleep with a book under your pillow and the words would soak into your brain and you would understand about isosceles triangles and Latin pluperfect.

After a while you take the treasure box and hide it where no one will find it. Especially not your father.

10

There was an askari — a guard — a tall thin Maasai, at the gate to the McMullens' old house.

'Is anyone home?' Ellie asked him. She could see sky through his earlobes. These had been stretched by heavy beads and copper coils.

He shook his head, his ear lobes jiggled.

'What time will they be back?'

'Badaai.' Later, he said. 'Labda saa kumi na moja.' Eleven o'clock. But she assumed he meant five, eleven being Swahili time, as the hours in East Africa begin at dawn.

It was just after three. She turned back to the taxi to wait. But then she reached inside her handbag, drew a five-hundred-shilling note into the palm of her hand.

'I just want to look at the garden,' she said, turning back to him. 'I used to know this place.'

Keeping her hand low she pressed the money through the wire mesh of the gate. He took it and opened the gate.

Ellie walked up the driveway, bordered by roses. As it always had been. She walked around the house. There were no toys in the garden, no chairs on the veranda. She suspected the tenants were Europeans on a short contract, two years, maybe, and this was where they slept and ate, never quite unpacking before packing again and moving on to some other World Bank or UN El Dorado.

No one had lived here properly since the McMullens. No one had tried to mark their presence in the garden. The flowerbeds were the same, the square agapanthus beds, a dispirited rock garden, a birdbath without water. Mrs McMullen had never taken an interest in her garden, or in anything besides Nina that Ellie could remember. Besides Nina and John Cameron. She looked up at the house, the dead windows, and half expected to see Mrs McMullen looking out, her sad face, the cool darkness behind her hiding her twisted child.

Beyond the garden, the vegetation turned ragged. Her garden and the McMullens' garden had both edged here into the wild and still did. Not much of it was left, perhaps a half-acre strip. Things had shifted, trees had moved and grown. Was the tree still there after all? How would she recognize it?

The tree had been special — sacred — because she had buried other things there, a mouse-bird that flew into the French doors and died, a mongoose that drowned in the kitchen drain.

The ground was dry as tinder underfoot, her feet padding on dead leaves and fallen twigs. Through the trees she could see the high fence of a new housing estate where once there had been only more trees. The new houses went on and on, replicating each other.

And then she found the tree. It had a hollow, clean through, about three feet from the base. Ellie used to think it was like an altar, and there she would put flowers and bird feathers, coloured stones and chrysalises. She hadn't believed in magic — even then she'd known bird feathers and dried flowers had no power, were only discarded or dead — but the beauty of small things had astounded her. The ribs of leaves. The feathers of a malachite kingfisher, like shards of sky.

There had been solace in beauty, she could touch it, and be safe and reassured in this quiet place where grown-ups never ventured. Even now the canopy above her swayed softly in the breeze and cobwebs trapped light in the lower branches.

She found a flat rock and used it as a shovel to dig around the base of the tree. The earth was dry and hard-packed. She kept digging until the edge of the box appeared and she gave a laugh of triumph. She had finally found tangible evidence of her being here. This old wood, this piece of her life, made it all true, not just dream or memory. Quickly, she scraped the earth from around the old cigar box and pulled it loose. She opened the lid.

Inside was a velvet ribbon rotted through, a lion's tooth, a bell from the collar of the cat that died, her Brownie pin for First Aid, cowrie shells, a scallop shell, and yes, Mrs McMullen's letter, fragile as ancient parchment.

Carefully, she unfolded the letter. And held it up to the light.

But there was only the palest of blue smudges, not even the definition of a word, let alone a sentence. Rain and the passing years had soaked the writing away.

Around her the late-afternoon sun filtered through the gum trees. The askari stood on the lawn, his newspaper under his arm, watching her without interest, perhaps just for something to do. Ellie wondered why she cared, why she was here with dirt under her fingernails. She'd wanted to know what Eileen McMullen had written — an accusation or declaration? Perhaps just a shopping list, after all. *Why* did it matter, a woman dead for almost three decades, the fact of her death unalterable. The truth of her death would change nothing. And I already know the truth, Ellie thought, I know he killed her.

As she walked back up the garden, towards the front gate, the askari shadowing her, she realized that what she was seeking was not Mrs McMullen but her father. Who was he that he had killed a woman? And got away with it? She had been wrong when she'd surmised that he was nothing to do with her. She had inherited his crime, not just his wide jaw, his cool eyes, his money. What he had done belonged to her, no murderer's child could ever disassociate herself from her father's actions; guilt is not absolved through birth or death, it breaches generations like disease. She had never been an innocent child.

11

A butter sculpture of a giraffe rose from the centre of the buffet. A young French couple were laughing at it. So gauche, they said, *du buerre*! Perhaps in ice it would have been elegant. A German couple, retired, were taking pictures of it, admiring the artistry, which was evident in the slow curve of the neck, the wide, expressive eyes, the knife edge of leg tendons. They were discussing with the Americans in their group the possibility that the sculptor was creating from memory, from his experience with giraffes and other wild animals, perhaps as a child in the bush.

Ellie suspected that the sculptor, like many Kenyans, had never seen a real giraffe. His talent was for still life, his art was imagination. For, unless he came from a rich family, how could he afford to travel to the game parks with the entry fees, hotels, fuel costs?

At the table next to her sat delegates from a water conference. She glanced at a portfolio leaning against a briefcase: 'Securing Clean Water in Rural Areas by 2005.' This is it, she thought, the best we can do. Some taps for the Africans in Kakamega while we irrigate golf courses in the Arizona desert.

She looked again at the giraffe. What will happen to it, she wondered. Will it go rancid? Or will the kitchen staff recycle it into neat little butter dishes? And just how much butter is it anyway? The giraffe seemed a testament to decadence, to how much could be so recklessly discarded.

What can I do, she thought. How can I make it fair, or even a tiny bit less unfair? Can I take it and give it to the glue boys, to the AIDS victims in the park? I could buy bread. We could make sandwiches. We could have a picnic. And tomorrow everyone would be hungry again.

★　★　★

Her immaculate bed was turned down. On the white sheets — sheets whiter and softer than any glue boy could dream — lay an envelope from reception. Inside, the documents from Richard Boudreau. She put it aside, switched on the TV, but there was just noise, babble, some foreign world where you always got what you deserved, prison or love, death or happiness.

She stood up, walked to the window and pulled back the curtains. She wanted to not be here, to be anywhere else, to be back with Peter, safe in his arms. To have another life, to be someone else, someone who could have stayed and loved. She wanted to be outside. But where could she go? Walk around Nairobi at night. Take a taxi, perhaps, drive out somewhere. But the hotel didn't recommend it, there were car-jackers, bandits, rapists. She pressed her hands against the window, feeling the warmth of the night through the glass.

Reflected in the window she could see the envelope. The contents gave her three million dollars in an account in the Channel Islands. He was good with money, oh yes, that thin Scottish blood had pulsed through a brain that knew how to add and subtract. What had Julius Mwangi said? 'And your father stealing from us. One set of accounts for his clients, another for the government.' How did he get the money out? Kenya had strict laws regarding the transfer of funds out of the country. Did he travel with false-bottomed suitcases? Smuggle gems? Tape banknotes to his torso? She could almost laugh — it seemed ridiculous.

But what did she know of him? His violence, his unpredictability. Everything else was mystery. Everything else was possible.

The cardboard box was in its corner, facing the wall in mute shame. She rifled through it again, the *Playboys*, Jesus, how pathetic, and why had 1988 been a particularly good year for the *Economist*? Hadn't it been the opposite? The end of Reagan and Thatcher. The restaurant receipt from the Hilton for June 1989 noted a pepper steak and a chicken Kiev, plus drinks, assorted, amounting to twice the cost of the meal. She imagined him drunk — no, she remembered him, how his eyes narrowed and his jaw slackened after so many whiskies, how he could be affectionate or dismissive or savage. She could never tell, his expression was the same, loving or hitting.

Across the bottom of the receipt he had written: 'Salim Rajiv'. The handwriting was his. She recognized the tiny, controlled print.

What did she want? An explanation from a dead man? A clue in a box of junk to the purloined millions? Let it go, she said to herself, let it go like everything else. Give the money away, go back. To Denver or Beaumont or Georgia.

Ellie turned back to the window. Out in the street, under the glow of one of the few working streetlights, she saw a clutch of ragged children. They were lifting up the sewer grating, they were slipping into the hole like TV spies. They're coming here, she thought, into the hotel compound, to the dumpsters behind the kitchen that the guests never see, and they will be licking butter from their filthy hands after all.

★ ★ ★

Nairobi's Hall of Records was built by the British colonial administration and it struck Ellie as a daring design: a solid square block with a façade of concrete lace stars. It was somewhere between Art Deco and Hindu Temple with Frank Lloyd Wright thrown in, and not at all what you would expect as a home for pen-pushing bureaucrats.

Inside there were sky-blue walls and cupolas, pure Georgian England. But instead of men in elegant breeches and velvet waistcoats moving quietly between ordered oak desks who must have inspired the decor, there was a maze of partitions, a floor stained with red earth, layers of fingerprints on every surface. Several dozen Africans milled around in an open area in front of the partitions. Ellie couldn't tell if they were waiting or if they worked here or if, perhaps, they were simply seeking shelter from the hard sunlight. Having waited for everything all their lives — buses, rain, jobs, important pieces of paper issued by government departments — they seemed beyond patience, like Zen monks who

116

can lower their heart rates to those of sleeping snakes.

Shelves of files breeched the walls, ten, twelve feet high. There was the musty smell of old paper and evaporating ink. She sensed the wild disorder behind the partitions as if it were a physical force, the centre of a galaxy of mislaid or mislabelled files that, like dishevelled stars, swung in elliptic, elusive orbits around the cupolas and blue walls.

As a child she had visited such government buildings on occasional errands with her mother — vaccination certificates, copies of birth certificates. There had been a hushed and serious atmosphere, neat queues and clean floors. Kenya was still a white man's country then, for at least a decade after independence. The whites still had the money, the education and the know-how that eluded — and had been systematically denied to — all but a handful of blacks. The Wazungu knew how to fly planes, run banks, remove tonsils, and operate lucrative safari outfits for the thousands of tourists who came to see the wonderland of Isak Dinesen and Ernest Hemingway. As Kenyans learned these same magic tricks of driving, doctoring, building, the influence of the wazungu began to wane. Kenyans stopped standing in arrow-straight queues just as they no longer stepped aside to let a white memsahib pass. Ellie wondered if the disorder was wilful, a reaction to the oppression of white rule, not just white law, but the minutiae of accompanying rules: which side to serve from, which side to clear from, which fork for the fish.

She had come to clock the distance between now and her flight that evening. She had come to this building out of a vague need for evidence of the past, like the name of an ancestor in a church register or on a tombstone: some part of me was here, she reasoned, recorded by someone who did not care enough to lie or fudge numbers. She stepped forward and asked the clerk behind the counter. He took the information she gave him and told her to wait. She sat on a bench beside an old man in a battered tweed jacket. How long had he been there, motionless, unblinking?

After some time the clerk returned to his counter, gesturing to her with a file. She took it and sat at a long wooden table and untied the narrow string that bound the faded yellow cardboard covers. Inside, a tedium of forms and letters — what had she expected? Still, here was her father's name and Donald Best listed as directors. Richard Boudreau as the company's advocate. The address of their office, Nanak House, a place she had never been, and Donald Best of whom she had no recollection, but who had existed, as confirmed on form 486.

Ellie filtered through the file and came to 'The Particulars of the Directors'. Here, her father had listed the other companies of which he held directorships. There were ten. She wrote these down and asked the clerk for the files. He took some time but eventually came back.

'Some are missing,' he said. 'We are computerizing and files are being moved around.' He had found seven. He added, 'But sometimes, the files are put away in the wrong location. There are people working here who are lazy and do not care.' His tone was informative but not apologetic: the problem of lost files was nothing to do with him.

She read through the files and there emerged a pattern of names, a loose weave of partnerships and shareholders, European names, Asian names, African names. Salim Rajiv appeared twice, as a partner in Linkoni Investments and a shareholder in Salaam Exports. The Mombasa-based Linkoni professed to 'Import Spare Parts for Heavy Machinery'; Salaam exported peanuts and dried fruit. Other names reoccurred in the myriad of companies: Bernard Harrison,

Simon Forbes, Edward Gecaga, Robert Wambugu, Sonya Valetine. There were dozens, perhaps a hundred names all told. Ellie knew that if she went on looking through the files the weave of names would tighten. But why, and into what design?

★　★　★

Outside, she hailed a taxi whose driver jumped every light, like a desperate refugee flinging himself onto the deck of a departing ship. He took her to Bindas Street, a dusty road behind the mosque. Here Nairobi stops pretending to be a proper city and becomes a third-world backwater of narrow side streets lined with rotting garbage and dukhas selling plastic shoes and fuzzy steering wheel covers. Ellie's taxi slalomed around the potholes and the Muslims in white futas or black arbayas.

The shop-front for Salaam Exports was filthy, shrouded by a crumbling arcade of long-faded peach paint. Ellie told the driver to wait and entered the shop. For a moment she stood still while her eyes adjusted to the gloom. There was a sack of peanuts in the corner.

Behind the counter sat an old Indian man with thick white hair and red teeth, stained by betel-nut juice. He looked at her through

Coke-bottle thick glasses. 'Can I help you, madam?'

'I'm looking for Salim Rajiv.'

'Present and accounted for, madam.'

'My father was in business with you.'

He frowned, confused, trying to place her. 'John Cameron. I'm Eleanor Cameron.'

'Oh, yes,' he said, extending a surprisingly smooth hand. 'Mr C. Yes, yes, we were partners for a long time, oh a long long time, twenty years. And you are his daughter? Well, well. But he was selling up to me maybe ten years ago, and I think I read that he has now passed on, as is God's will, so I am sorry for your loss.'

'He was a partner in this business?'

'Oh yes, he was beginning it with me,' Mr Rajiv said, smiling.

'And what kind of business is it?'

'We are exporting peanuts and dried fruits.' He saw her looking at the single bag of peanuts. 'We keep our stock in the warehouse location. This is just our town office. But is this your question?'

She said: 'Why was my father exporting peanuts? He was an accountant.'

'It's a very good business, madam. He was a very clever man, your father, an excellent head for business.'

She tried to think of her father sitting in

here in the cramped dark with Mr Rajiv. 'Was this how he got money out of the country?'

Mr Rajiv puffed himself up, an ego inflated by a bicycle pump. 'What are you implying, madam? I'm not certain what it is you seek by coming here.'

'It's just he was involved in all these odd companies — peanuts, beer, shoes, cars, tractor parts. I'm just trying to understand why — what it was all about.'

Mr Rajiv sighed, deflating. He couldn't be bothered to take offence any longer. 'Poor dear. I remember now. He told me about you once, how you were in America. And at the time I thought this was a very good thing, an education in America for a child. I sent my own son to England. But it is very sad, a sad thing for a father.'

Ellie looked at him, 'Did he say he was sad?'

'No, no, goodness no. Your father was a very private man.' He gestured for her to come behind the counter with him, where there was another stool. 'You want something? A Pepsi? Tea?'

'No, thank you.'

He nodded, 'Okay, so you think Mr C and I are doing some illegal things?'

'He was a rich man. He got that way somehow.'

'Okay. But you understand that these are not illegal things in our countries, only here because of the stupid mentality, oh, the way to make foreign exchange is to keep it, to lock it up. Oh dear me no! The way to make foreign exchange is to create a good investment environment, such as roads and 24-hour electricity and not so many hooligans stealing cars and killing people. But the problem with that is the bloody thieving politicians must be doing something with the government's money, what all these silly donors, the World Bank and so on are giving them, instead of just lining their own pockets. The laws are different now in modern Kenya — ' he said 'modern' with raised eyebrows ' — but before, before? No, no, only a few hundred shillings you were allowed to take out, enough to buy you a tube fare from Oxford Street to Victoria Station.'

He looked at her to make sure she was understanding him: Salim Rajiv and John Cameron had been victims of circumstance and bad governance. 'My family lost everything in Uganda,' he said. '1972. One day we have a good business in Kampala and Gulu and Busia, paint and hardware and so forth, the next day we are here in Nairobi with two suitcases between ten of us and the kids crying and making one hell of a racket. So I said to my wife Meena, 'Meena', I said, 'We make our home here but we make our bank someplace else. We're not having these bloody thieving Africans steal all our money again.' So you see, we are selling peanuts to Japan, but also flowers, bananas and some meat products to other countries, to Greece, Italy, France, Finland.'

He handed her some peanuts, 'See, they are very good.'

'But how do you take money out of the country? Even if you sell them there, you have to be paid here, in Kenyan currency.'

'Which is bloody worthless!' He laughed and cracked open a peanut. 'We are under-invoicing, you see. We are saying the peanuts are worth five shillings a kilo, but we are selling them in Japan for seven shillings a kilo. The difference is paid to us in yen in Japan. When you are exporting many tons of peanuts, the two shillings is becoming a goodly amount. Now, your father was also doing this for hotels and safari camps. Charging fifty dollars a night on the books here, but the real price is one hundred dollars a night, and the extra fifty, you see, is paid in Europe.

'This is very common. But your father was a kind of genius. He had maybe two hundred companies, all of them under-invoicing for exports or over-invoicing for imports. For instance, we are importing generators from Germany. We say these generators are worth two thousand dollars, but in fact we are only paying fifteen hundred dollars for them in Germany. So we are keeping the five hundred in Germany. And there is also real estate. The worth of land is much more than you pay here because you pay the balance in Switzerland. On and on.'

Mr Rajiv spread his upturned palms and smiled, 'And this is how he was getting people's money out, through these transactions. Then deducting a commission for himself, for his own account in the UK. Poetry. I tell you, poetry.'

'What if someone had found out?'

'Oh, well, they care an awful lot if they are finding out and not also making something for themselves. But your father, he knew everyone, you see, how they fiddle their accounts, all the MPs, the big boys, everyone, he was helping them all get money out.'

'Powerful people?'

Mr Rajiv tapped his nose. 'You know these Wabenzi.'

She didn't know.

'With their flats in London and Paris, their children in the Swiss boarding school,' he said. 'The tribe of the Mercedes Benz

— Wabenzi. Mr C knew them, yes indeed. Oh, he was a clever man, your father. And very private, not telling anyone, you see, so they trusted him.'

Ellie thanked him for his time and picked up her bag. As she reached the door, about to step into the white midday light, she said, 'Did you like him?'

'Oh, clever, as I say, clever, clever.'

'That's not what I asked.'

'It was not for me to think about. We were strictly business. But he was always treating me with manners, you know, not like some bloody dirty Indian.'

Outside, the sun startled her and she closed her eyes for a moment. Poetry. She'd never credited John Cameron with an imagination but now she wondered at the warrens of his mind, the man concocting this poetry of numbers, of schemes.

⋆ ⋆ ⋆

At the hotel, Ellie was packing her one small suitcase. On the handle was a tangle of old airline and bus luggage tags, the places she had been. This was all that was left of them. Not friends, familiar voices down the phone, photographs or letters. Only abbreviations on a faded strip of paper. ABQ, LAX, DFW.

The bellboy appeared, glanced at the suitcase, and then around the room, 'Your bags, madam?'

'Just the one.'

He seemed disappointed, placing the solitary suitcase on the large brass trolley.

In the elevator, she glanced in the mirror, ran her fingers roughly through her hair, drawing the stray strands back into a clip. She was thinking of Vermont and the apple-green summer she might find waiting there, or Austin and a honky-tonk cold beer, a musician in a purple velvet suit. She was thinking of her reflection in some other future mirror, maybe New Orleans or Tuba City.

The lobby was crowded. A Baptist church group had just finished their seminar on 'Politics as a Subject for Sermons' and its members stood in clusters exchanging addresses and dinner plans. They were still winter-pale. After all, it was one thing to spend their congregation's money on a 200-dollar-a-night hotel in the name of helping their poor black brothers and sisters, but something else to return with a tropical tan. Ellie paid her bill and walked out into her final evening.

★   ★   ★

The worst of the traffic had passed but the air was heavy with smoky residue. The glue boys had retired for the day. Ellie looked out the taxi's window and saw them tussling on the roadside, ignoring her and the other motorists. She appreciated that they had a certain kind of freedom. The certainty of death fixed them entirely in the present.

The taxi took her away through the city's tattered outskirts, past the dusty people waiting for their buses in their cheap suits and re-soled shoes. In the distance, the Ngongs wavered in the last of the honey light. The knuckles of a giant, she remembered, he had fallen and the earth had covered him silently as a blanket, and here was his fist, five ridges notching the sky. As a child, she'd walked up there with school friends. She'd run along the path that linked the crests: how far apart those ridges had suddenly seemed, and the further you went the more uncertain the path became until it was just a game trail whispering in the long grass. The wind had churned up from the dry red plains of the Rift Valley. Black-tailed hawks floated in the up-draughts and there were wild flowers and game, sometimes buffalo, and always giraffe and impala.

Now a host of radio towers clusters on the summit and no one walks up there anymore because of the bandits. The eastern slopes of the hills are covered with mealie patches and a flower farm belonging to the President's son squats like a spaceship where the deep, dark Ololua Forest had once been. The beauty had slipped away, like so much else, like everything else, in the wake of an airplane.

Ellie remembered now, with perfect clarity, her leaving all those years ago, looking through the oval porthole, watching the long, dry grass blur beyond the runway, and then rising up over Nairobi, the ragged city of beggar-boys and the smiling lepers of Bizarre Street. The plane had banked to the left over leopards in forests, over her house and Rosa and Baptist and the wide, lonely, lion-coloured land. Everything she knew, everything that was familiar, that was hers, had gone.

She leaned back against the taxi seat. She had not known, had not guessed, how much was gone for ever, her childhood abandoned like a barren claim. Or what it meant to lose so much. I didn't grieve because I didn't understand for ever and never. The garden of my childhood where butterflies hatched and small brown snakes sunbathed on brown earth is gone, she thought, so utterly that it is as if it never existed.

* * *

She was at the airport. She stepped out of the taxi and onto the kerb. It was dark now, the sky murky beyond the fluorescent lights. She reached into her bag for her money. The bills were in her hand, bright and crisp, bank-fresh, *Shillingi mia tano, shillingi elfu moja.* She was feeling already the rush and lift, the silence of passengers as the plane climbs, leaving, not yet arriving, still connected to those left behind, waving or weeping.

But when she tried to give the driver the money she found that she could not. She was thinking of the crosses on the roadsides in New Mexico, hung about with wreaths of plastic flowers to mark where someone had died. Certain crosses on certain roads became familiar to her. She could tell when the flowers had been replaced or some new memento added, a stuffed toy, a letter. The grief-stricken had come to remind themselves that the death had happened, had not been a dream or a mistake. The crosses marked endings.

Her own past was strewn about, littering the surface of this other country, and she knew now that she could not walk away until she had claimed it and buried it and marked it. She said to the taxi driver, 'Ninarudi.' Now I go back. And they drove back toward the city.

12

It was difficult to know what tone of voice to use with the servants. As mistress of the house, Helen now had three at her disposal. Sam, the cook, and Rosa, the housegirl (who would also be an ayah when the time came for children) had both been with John for some time. Pious, the gardener, had just been hired. They waited for instructions, Sam with his shoulders back like a soldier, Pious holding his red wool hat, looking down, his wide bare feet splayed out, as if flattened by a vehicle in the road, Rosa with her broom like a bayonet and her starched pink uniform. But Helen had never told anyone what to do.

She worried that they would find her weak and take advantage of her. Aunt B had warned against this: 'They'll always be trying one on. The important thing is to let them know who's in charge and that you won't stand for any nonsense.'

Aunt B dismissed her servants for minute infractions. 'Right,' she would say at the break of a glass or the drop of a soufflé. 'That's it, off you go.'

'But, memsahib,' would come the plaintive

reply and with it a forlorn expression, eyes like dinner plates, 'Iko shida kidogo.' There is a small problem. A dead brother, unpaid school fees.

'Kwenda, kwahiri.' Aunt B was unmoved, waving a hand in the air as if warding off a fly. Go, goodbye. 'They have so many problems,' she told Helen, 'And the second you try to help, well, their problems are yours. You have your own problems. And never, ever give them money. There will always be some sob story about a sick child, but it's either a lie or it doesn't matter. They have so many children, like rabbits, they die all the time. Death doesn't mean the same to them because they don't emotionally attach to their children the way we do.

'You must always remember about servants,' Aunt B further advised, 'There are plenty more out there, an endless supply. And every one as bad and useless as the last.'

Looking at the trio before her, Helen tried to imagine sacking them when she had trouble mustering the courage to tell them to fry eggs or water the roses.

'Sam,' she finally managed. She wanted to be brisk and efficient, impersonal. It was important not to get too fond of the servants because then you might trust them. Uncle Stanley told her to always remember the Mau

Mau. Remember the families killed at midnight, their throats cut, *even the children*, by trusted servants. Ayahs murdering the white babies in their care, swinging them in the air and dashing their heads against the floor, as if pounding millet. Remember what they did to their own people: tying them to the ground, covering them with honey and leaving them for the Siafu ants. Remember they are wicked and shiftless.

Helen said, 'Tonight we'll have steak and kidney pie with vegetables. What vegetables do we have?'

'We have spinach and carrot, memsahib.'

'Right. That will be fine.' She looked at Rosa. 'Rosa, can you polish the silver today?' Rosa nodded. 'And Pious, I don't know much about the garden. What do you think needs to be done?'

Pious smiled and said nothing.

'Pious?' she tried again, 'The garden? Do we need to plant anything? Cut anything down?'

Pious smiled on.

'He does not know English,' Sam said with triumph. 'Only Kikuyu and some small Swahili.' He said Kikuyu like a dirty word.

Helen looked out at the garden. It was a jungle. Even the domestic English plants looked like mad vines growing on Venus. She thought of her mother's careful herbaceous borders and ordered rose garden, the rockery and the lily pond. 'Ask him,' she said, then remembering Aunt B, '*Tell* him just to make everything a bit neater — 'safi'.'

Sam nodded and said something to Pious in Swahili. Pious snapped his heals together and saluted her. 'Sawa sawa, memsahib!'

That done, Helen left the kitchen and walked upstairs. She loved the house, with its big rooms and light. John had told her she could 'redecorate', which made her smile to herself because there was very little decoration in the whole house. 'Decorate' was more like it. The rooms only had beds, not even bedspreads. The sitting room consisted of old sofas and a chair — bachelor decor. She was glad his ex-wife hadn't lived here with him, that this house was not haunted by her failure and her taste.

Five bedrooms, four bathrooms, two drawing rooms, a dining room, study and ten acres. Helen would make it lovely. There were fabrics in the dukhas on Bazaar Street, Egyptian cottons, Jinja cottons, silks from India and China, colour and texture. There were fundis who could make slipcovers and bed covers and furniture, whatever she wanted, beds, tables, bookcases from mahogany or ebony or mavuli. She would fill the house with beauty, with light, with children.

She fanned out the colour swatches. With all the sunlight, this room could take cool colours, a cool blue or a pale yellow. The yellow was less expensive, so she favoured it. John was careful about money — that was his business. He gave her a monthly allowance in cash, which wasn't very much, really, but most things she bought on account. At the end of the month she and John would go through the accounts. Sometimes he would question her purchases, saying the meat was too expensive or not to buy mangoes out of season. Once she put a lipstick on account at the chemist's. He told her such a purchase should come out of her cash allowance. 'I'm trying to teach you about household finances,' he said. 'So many women don't know how to handle money. It's important that you learn.' So she paid attention.

After they'd gone over the purchases on account, they would go over the cash allowance purchases. He liked her to keep receipts for these purchases as well, even a cup of coffee at the Thorn Tree. If she'd bought a lipstick last month she couldn't very well buy another one this month without looking frivolous. Finally, John would note everything neatly in a ledger marked 'Household Accounts' and then she'd sign off at the bottom of the page. It was all very professional. He'd told her to come up with a budget for the decoration and she was determined to do him proud.

But now she could hear an argument outside, men shouting at each other in Swahili, a woman trying to break it up. The noise was coming from near the huge monkey puzzle tree behind the kitchen. Helen rushed downstairs, outside.

She found them there by the tree, Sam and Pious shouting at each other, Rosa trying to push them apart.

'What's the matter?' Helen said. She remembered how Uncle Stanley stood with his hands on his hips when he was angry with his workers, so she did this now. More than anything it reassured her, as if she was anchoring herself, so her hands wouldn't flutter in a feminine, useless way.

Sam and Pious said nothing, so Helen looked to Rosa. 'Tell me what's going on.'

Rosa raised her eyebrows and pointed to Sam. 'He is a Luo,' and pointed at Pious, 'and he is a Kikuyu.' This was supposed to make sense, Helen was supposed to understand this code. If she didn't they would know she was hopeless. They would laugh behind her back

136

and steal the sugar. She looked at Rosa, 'And you?'

'I am a Luhya and a Christian,' Rosa said with pride.

'Right,' said Helen sternly. 'If there is any more fighting I will have to speak to the Bwana and there will be trouble for all of you.'

Of course she couldn't because he'd left the running of the house entirely to her. But at least the servants looked chastened.

It was only later when she heard the sound of an axe and looked out the window and saw Pious chopping down the monkey puzzle tree that Rosa's explanation 'Pious is Kikuyu and Sam is Luo' meant that they hated each other. Sam had translated to Pious the wrong instructions on purpose, and Pious, suspicious of this, had accused him thus, and so the fight began.

It was also later when the carrots and vegetables were served inside a pastry crust for dinner. There was no steak and kidney, just the pie. She was so ashamed, but John laughed gently, 'You'll get the hang of it.' She confronted Sam. He told her, 'But there was no nyama.'

'No what?'

'No meat, memsahib.'

She said, 'But why didn't you tell me?'

He said nothing, as if he couldn't hear her or as if she was speaking Greek. He moved his right foot in a small circle on the floor. She thought: he's not that stupid. He's taking the mickey.

But Eileen confirmed what B had said: 'They *are* that stupid. They're children. They can't plan anything. They can't keep track of anything. They'll only notice the sugar is running low when it's run out completely — even if they've taken it themselves. You have to think of everything. You have to do their thinking for them.'

The butter ran out, the shirts were over-starched, and you couldn't trust them with a bottle of bleach. Eileen and the other women didn't mind talking about these problems when they came for coffee. In fact, sitting on the veranda of a morning, refreshing their Yardley lipstick and snacking on Sam's waferlight shortbread, it was almost all they talked about. Helen knew she was expected to contribute in kind. And it didn't matter if Sam or Rosa was near by because these were facts being discussed, not insults. It wasn't personal.

Helen also learned that there were tribal categories for servants. The Maasai were lazy but made good askaris, the Luhyas made the best nannies, the Kamba the best gardeners,

Luos were too arrogant for their own good. And the 'Kyukes' — the Kikuyus — they were sharp as tacks, good businessmen, good thieves, you had to keep an eye on them. After all, President Kenyatta was a Kikuyu and wasn't he a wily old fox.

13

'Tell him we met on the plane,' Ellie said to the secretary.

It was morning, the next day. She had ordered room service for breakfast, and was standing by the open window watching the happy clappers erect their tent in the park below. God will save us, they were singing. God will promote us to glory.

Julius Mwangi came on the line, 'Hello? Are you the lady who was sitting next to me?'

'Yes, Eleanor Cameron.'

'And how are you? Enjoying Nairobi?'

'It's fine, yes, thank you. Mr Mwangi — '

'Julius, please.'

'Julius, I have some legal questions and I wondered if I could make an appointment with you. I won't need much of your time.'

'I'm sorry. I'm very booked up at the moment.'

'Could you recommend someone? It's just a few questions.'

He took a moment to consider. 'Can you meet me for coffee in an hour? Say ten-thirty? I'm between court appointments.' Then he gave her the address, a local café in the city centre.

She was on time but he was waiting and rose to greet her. He wore an impeccable suit, a white raw-silk shirt with French cuffs — none of which could be purchased locally — any more than expensive hospital care in London for his mother. She wondered, then, how he got his money out, what secrets he traded or kept.

He looked expectantly at her, impatient. She sat down.

'I think my father may have murdered a woman. A long time ago, in 1974.'

Julius raised his eyebrows, exhaled. 'There's no statute of limitations on murder. You are looking to prosecute?'

'He died a few months ago. The woman was his mistress, she'd been strangled. It was supposed to be a suicide. But it wasn't.'

'You were a witness?'

'I found the body. He'd just been there with her, and the servants — ' She stopped, suddenly aware of the word 'servant'; it seemed a racial and social anachronism. But Julius hadn't noticed, he probably had servants of his own. She went on, 'The house staff said there had been an argument.'

'And why do you believe it was a murder?'

'He was a violent man,' she said, and

141

could see his hands pressing over Eileen McMullen's face, blotting her out.

The waitress brought the coffee. Julius noted a circle of lipstick on the rim of his cup and gestured to her. 'Take it away.'

The waitress looked embarrassed. 'I will bring you another.'

'No, no,' he said and made a shooing motion with his hands. 'Just take it away.' He turned to Ellie, 'If there was any doubt about the circumstances of her death, surely there would have been an inquest.'

'My father had powerful allies,' she said. 'He could easily have made sure her death was ruled a suicide.'

'Easily?' Julius cocked his head. 'Even friends want something for their co-operation. Favours, kickbacks, money. The usual.'

'He could have done that,' she said.

'No one who would have questioned the verdict?' Julius said.

Ellie thought of Dr McMullen. She'd seen him running from his car into the house, his thin grey hair swept up off his forehead by the wind into an odd little peak, like a horn. He was a kind man, he always had sweets in his pocket for her. But she had no memory of him after Mrs McMullen's death.

'I don't know,' she said. 'Her husband, maybe. But I don't think so. He lived next door. If there had been a fuss I think I would have known.'

For a moment Julius said nothing, and then raised his eyes to hers. 'I don't understand. Why does this matter, twenty, thirty years later? I think you will be disappointed and you won't find your answer.'

'I need to try.'

'Perhaps the police records of the incident will reveal something. Perhaps there was an inquest. You should find them with CID. They keep all murders and suicides, cases of special interest, in perpetuity. Ask for Dorothy in archives. Tell her I sent you.'

He shifted to reach for his wallet. He wasn't interested in her story. She wanted him to be, she wanted it to matter.

'It's just the corruption involved, if he did do it, a white man using his power to twist the law,' she said.

'That isn't corruption, my dear woman.' He put two hundred shillings on the table and stood. 'And he was white. So what? It matters to you wazungu, not to us. Still the same stories again and again about old murders, rich whites killing each other, drinking too much, screwing their friends' wives. My God, who cares? Africans die by the thousands every day!'

When he laughed she glimpsed someone else, a younger man with humour and hope. Then he looked at her. 'As for corruption, corruption is when thousands of people starve to death because some politician has stolen their land or their grain. Corruption is what we do to each other, we Africans, this is our self-mutilation.' He waved his hand, a courtroom gesture that might indicate either outrage or the futility of giving a shit. Either way, false dramatics by a man Ellie suspected no longer knew, or cared, where the law began and ended.

★ ★ ★

Ellie looked out the taxi window and thought, nothing stays new in this country. All it takes is a rainy season's worth of footprints and red mud stains the floor. All it takes is a drought and the pavements crack and the dust rises up in great, whirling devils cloaking everything, waiting to turn to blood-red mud in the rain. The sun cracks windows and roads, the wind blows down the telephone lines and buildings tilt or fray.

And today, the Maasai were grazing their cattle and their goats with rattling bells on the roundabout.

It wasn't just the natives the colonial administration had tried to control but the very nature of the continent: the voodoo weather, the boisterous biology of all living things. For a while, they had succeeded and laid down the ordered avenues of old Nairobi, the immaculate roundabouts and shady arcades. It seemed as if someone had dreamed of Chiswick and then built it in the middle of the Athi Plains, a colonial folly lacking imagination and grandeur, the folly of middle-class bank clerks and women who wore lead weights in their hems and sought safety in the familiar. They had their Sunday God and their triplicate forms, their club rules, the tightly packed layers of their hierarchy, goodness, rightness, laundry detergent and sponge cake with jam filling for tea. But none of it could stand up to a herd of hungry goats with sharp, muddy hooves and barefoot herders who wore coloured beads on their wrists. Isn't that what they'd always said as a joke, and then in all seriousness on Independence Day? 'AWA.' Africa Wins Again.

She left the taxi and walked through the gates of Nairobi's Criminal Investigation Department. She was now used to the clutter of people with their indeterminate aims who chatted in small groups or waited on uneven

145

benches. They looked at her with intense suspicion. A mzungu at CID could only be making trouble for some African. She had come, surely, to press charges against her housegirl or cook for stealing sugar or some gin from a bottle that had been secretly marked to catch the perpetrator. As she crossed the courtyard toward the archives building she passed a prisoner in a ragged uniform and bare feet sweeping leaves. He glanced up at her with yellow eyes and impenetrable pupils. Who was he, what had he done? In the labyrinth of third world justice was he guilty? Or just poor?

★ ★ ★

'Is it possible to see a police report from the seventies, a suicide?' she asked Dorothy. Dorothy was a stout, middle-aged woman in a plain dress and low-heeled shoes. Several tears in the dress had been carefully repaired. Her desk seemed to retreat against the window under the aggressive advance of ranks of metal shelves.

'You have a date? At least the month or even the year? The district?' Dorothy was already pushing her chair back. 'We have too many files, you see, too many deaths. People killing themselves or each other. Some days I

146

feel I am surrounded by misfortune and weakness.'

'1974. Kitisuru. I think.'

Ellie waited at Dorothy's table. There were other files, pending placement back on the shelves. Ellie opened the top one: a Frenchman had killed a Somali girl in Malindi, a coastal resort town. He had met her in a bar, there had been some sort of argument back in the hotel room, he had smashed her head in, wrapped her in the bed sheets and dumped her on the roadside twenty miles south of town. Ellie read on. While the Frenchman had admitted to the crime, he claimed to have been so drunk he could not remember. But a witness in the room next door remembered — remembered hearing the Somali girl say, 'Sitaki, sitaki.' He remembered hearing her crying, repeating the mantra of her despair, 'Sitaki.' I don't want, I don't want. After a brief trial, there had been a sentence: eighteen months' imprisonment. But even this had been suspended. It was clear: the worth of a Somali whore was only what you paid her on the bed; the worth of a judge what you paid him under the table. The worth of a mzungu was the size of his wallet.

Dorothy came back with a filing box. 'It should be in here. You can look for yourself.'

It was the third file down, case KA251–34.

147

Ellie read the incident report: the death of Eileen McMullen on October 2, 1974 at 513 Upper Kabete Road, Kitisuru. The 38-year-old British woman's cause of death appeared to be strangulation, self-inflicted with the belt of her dressing gown, as indicated by the angle of the ligatures on the neck. The investigating officer was Lt Patrick O'Shea of the CID. Baptist Karabillo, a Luhya and an employee of the McMullen household, had been taken in for questioning and held for forty-eight hours. He was released at the request of his employer, Dr Roy McMullen.

There had been no inquest. The postmortem had confirmed death by suicide. The brief witness statements given by her mother, her father, Roy McMullen and another neighbour confirmed Eileen's sad and unstable mental condition, her unsurprising end. Baptist's statement was not included, nor Rosa's — if they had even been asked to give them. What they saw and heard never counted for much.

Eileen was a sad woman who'd killed herself. Everyone could send flowers and wash the soil of her grave from their hands. Not so much older than me, Ellie thought, someone I might meet at a cocktail party, someone even now I wouldn't like. She could see Mrs McMullen in her floaty dress shouting at Baptist, a broken glass near his bare feet: 'Clean it up!' Even remembering now, Ellie felt the shame of the moment for Baptist, but also for herself because she did not go to him, she stayed on the sofa beside her mother with a biscuit and milky tea. Baptist did not look at her, he never did when they were inside Mrs McMullen's house, only out behind the kitchen with the radio when he would teach her Christian songs.

She put the forms back in their file.

But a small note torn from a spiral pad slipped loose, fluttered to the floor face down. Someone had written: 'Naivasha — July 6, 1960.'

★   ★   ★

She asked Dorothy to look for the date. Perhaps there was a file. Dorothy consulted her ledger, and yes, there was the record of a file, a murder, case number NV421–B. But when she went to look for the file it wasn't there.

14

The McMullens always come over for Sunday lunch. They used to bring Nina when she was a baby, when she would sleep right through, before she moaned and cried all the time. Mum tries to make you go over and play with Nina, but Nina can't play, she can't even sit up. Her head is wobbly.

Sometimes she screams and has these fits and Mrs McMullen has to hold her down and put a pill in her mouth. Once, when they come for lunch, Nina has one of her fits and Dr McMullen has to run home and get the pills. Your father helps Mrs McMullen hold Nina down.

Who would have thought she had any strength in those bird-leg limbs, but she thrashes and thrashes like someone drowning.

'Sssshhhh, sshhhhh,' Mrs McMullen keeps on saying. 'It's okay, it's okay.'

'Jesus Christ,' your father says. He doesn't like noise and Nina is making a lot of it. But he doesn't seem angry about the noise, he seems surprised.

'Is there anything I can do?' Mum says. She is standing to the side and you can tell she is frightened, her hand is over her open mouth.

Nina won't stop screaming, not with pain like getting in the bath with bad grazes on your knees, but something else. And it isn't okay, you can see that. It will never be okay. Maybe that's what Nina is screaming about, she knows what she is. You would scream if you were like that. Or like the children on Bizarre Street who try to touch you with their lobster-claw hands. Alison Chester told you their parents made them like that on purpose so they could beg for a living — it's the only hope they have. You don't believe her, it's impossible, mothers breaking their babies' legs and bending them the wrong way so they must shuffle on the ground for their whole lives. They wear flip-flops on their hands and tie cardboard to their knees and they crawl after you smiling, 'Rafiki, saidia, rafiki.' Some of the grown-up beggars are lepers and they try and touch you. If they touch you you will get leprosy and your nose and fingers will fall off and you will smell like compost. Every morning you wake up and check to see if your nose is still there.

Nina's dress rides up her thighs and you can see she is wearing baby nappies even though she is seven. Older than you. Dr McMullen comes running back with the pills, his face red and puffing. He forces the pills down her throat, like Mum does with the dogs, and after a few more minutes Nina is quiet and still.

Mrs McMullen sits on the floor and starts to cry. You had never seen a grown-up cry and you want to watch but your father says: 'Up to your room!' You don't move right away, not fast enough, and so your father comes and slap, hard on your thighs with his hand. It feels like pins jabbing and diamonds sparkling under your skin, but it is your face that burns.

Some time later Nina goes home to England. How can she go home if her mother and father are still here? 'She needs special care,' Mum explains. She is going to A Home, not home. A Home is like a hospital.

You wonder why Mrs McMullen keeps Nina's room so perfectly. You spy on Mrs McMullen through the windows and know she is in there every day arranging the dolls Nina never played with, not before, not now and not any time soon. Why doesn't she give them to you?

One Sunday before Nina went away and after she had her bad fit that made Mrs McMullen cry, Mum goes up for a sleep after lunch. Dr McMullen is called away on an emergency. Mrs McMullen is taking a long time finishing her coffee, Nina is sleeping.

Your father says, 'Eleanor, go out and play.' You do what he says right away, you run outside and down to the sandpit.

Play, he told you, so you play. You throw sand up in the air, you run around and around the sandpit, you swing on the swings. And when you've played, as you've been told, you go back up to the house, very quietly. You think, you feel, there is some secret your father is hiding.

In the living room you see Nina still sleeping in the corner. Her dress is so pretty, dark pink velvet with smocking, and her tights are white lace, like you've always wanted.

There is no one in the kitchen, just the clean glasses drying on the sideboard, for Sam has gone off for the afternoon and Rosa is always off all day on Sundays. You look in the window of your father's study, that room forbidden to you. You see them, but also cannot see them, just some blurred form of them as if your eyes won't focus on what they don't want to see. Mrs McMullen sitting on your father's desk, with her legs open. And yet you see very clearly her pearl earrings. How the sun sparkles on them. Drops of rain.

And how she sees you.

You run. Down to the bottom of the garden. You climb into the sacred tree, high into the branches where you can see the whole garden. You are breathless, gulping air, bats flapping in your heart. Your father comes out of the house. He looks around but he doesn't call your name. Because you are invisible he goes back into the house.

What must you do? You can run away, you can go and live with Rosa's children in Kisumu and go to an African school and eat posho every day. You can be adopted by another family and move to Australia. You can think of a dozen different places, but after all, whatever you do he will find you. You might be walking on the side of the road and a police car will slow down. You might walk into the forest and the leopard will be waiting. There is nowhere you can go, only the place of fear, the shadows in the hallway with long fingers that tangle in your hair. They can slip under the bottom of the door or through a crack in the window.

That night Mum says, kiss your father goodnight and you do. He rustles the pages of his magazine. But after you go to bed, you hear him coming up the stairs, the footfalls to your door. You jump out of bed and run across your room to the cupboard. Far back behind the clothes, in the pitch-dark, witch-dark you hide, and you can hear him and see what he is seeing, as if by magic his eyes are yours. He is checking under the bed, and you are not there, so he comes towards the cupboard, one foot then the other, five giant steps across the floor.

He finds you and pulls you out. Still you do not open your eyes, do not want to see the monster's face though his dragon breath singes your hair.

'Eleanor,' he says. He is holding you by the arms, matchsticks in his hands. 'You are to say nothing about what you saw this afternoon. Do you understand?'

Your eyes close tight, make it go away. He squeezes your arms so it hurts. Voice low to the ground like a snake: 'Do you understand?'

He steals even your silence from you.

'Yes,' you whisper.

15

The light licked the leaves of the pepper tree. The light scattered in freckles onto the white netting over the old black perambulator. The air was pepper-scented and the garden was full of birds.

Helen wondered at her daughter whose fists and feet had such latent power, whose whole body desired movement, as if she couldn't wait to run and dance. Helen watched Eleanor Penelope Cameron reach up for the light and the leaves with small, hungry hands.

Rosa came out and lifted Eleanor from the pram and held her up so the sun circled her blonde hair. 'Malaika, Malaika,' Rosa said. Angel, angel. Eleanor gave a little shriek of joy. 'This baby is strong with God's love.' Rosa handed the baby to Helen.

Opening her shirt, Helen fed Ellie. She felt the African sun on her breasts. Everything was right, everything was whole. This perfect moment.

16

D. Best was listed in the phone book. But a young woman with an Italian accent answered. 'Mr Best? No, no, he is not living here any more.'

'Do you know where I could find him?'

'This is still his house but a year ago he rents it to us because he was sick. He moves to some smaller place, with good security, you know, a place with other old people and I think some nurses. You know this place?'

'I'm sorry,' Ellie said. 'I don't.'

'Hold on. I ask my husband. I think one day he took some things there for Mr Best.'

A moment passed, the woman came back. 'Yes, he says the place is called Summer Field. Out past the airport, to Athi River.'

Ellie thanked her but before she hung up the woman said, 'He is not so good, his mind. It's difficult for him.'

The phone book yielded no Summer Field. But then she tried Somerfield. Somerfield Retirement Community, Athi River.

She found Eric, or he found her, waving and smiling from under the tree where he waited with the other taxi drivers.

'Madam,' he said, 'Where do we go today?'

The city no longer surrendered to the dry, yellow plains the way it once had, but lingered on with billboards and petrol stations, restaurants, a drive-in theatre, and a stinking meat-packing factory. The smell made Ellie think instantly of the terror of the cows, the press and panic, the blood-slippery floor.

The road forked right, the smell was gone, and now there were neat maisonettes on a hillside, the shambas of corn beside a dusty office complex with broken windows. Further on, she and Eric saw a small sign for Somerfield. At the gate, the guard looked at Eric and then at Ellie, and nodded. They drove through and up a drive lined with rosemary bushes. There was nothing quaint about the square, utilitarian buildings, the small windows and cement walkways, no pretence that this was anything but a place to wait for death. She could see some of the residents, sitting or tottering, white and white-haired, among the African nurses.

'What is this place?' Eric asked.

'It's a home for old people,' she said.

'They want to live here and not with their families?'

'They have no families,' she said. 'Or families who can't take care of them any more.' It was here, perhaps, that her father

158

would have been taken, or put, if anyone knew how he had been living. Maybe that was why he had kept his distance from the white community in the end, so he could die privately. As Salim Rajiv said, he was a private man.

The nurse at the front desk was very kind and led Ellie down a hallway. There was no luxury here, not much money, it was silent and lonely and stank of disinfectant and the wet-wool smell of old age. Mr Best was sitting by a window, looking out onto the dry garden. He was completely bald but for a few hairs around the base of his skull. He looked at her with marsh-brown eyes.

'I'm Eleanor Cameron,' she said. 'John Cameron's daughter.'

He said nothing. His face had been stilled by a stroke.

'I wanted to ask you about him,' she said, moving closer. There was nothing in his eyes. She glanced at the nurse, who shrugged, 'Sometimes he understands.' Then she left.

Ellie sat on the edge of the bed. 'Do you remember him?'

'John,' he said, neither a question nor an affirmation.

'Yes, John Cameron. You were partners.'

'Yes.' The same, flat tone.

'Did you know Eileen McMullen?'

Mr Best turned away now, looking out the window. 'She's not here. She died.'

'When did she die, Mr Best?'

'A few months ago. They are very careless here.'

'How did she die?'

'Her hip. She fell. They operated but they don't know what they're doing.'

'Who is this we're talking about?'

'Margaret.'

'No, I mean Eileen McMullen. Can you remember her, from a very long time ago, 1974?'

'Oh, yes.'

'She died.'

'He was a doctor. Roy.'

'Yes, that's right, Roy was her husband.' Ellie's heart skipped. He knew, he remembered, stumbling back through so many years, the narrow alleyways of his memory. She could lead him.

'Eileen and my father had an affair. Did you know?'

'They had an affair.'

She looked at him, the blank face, and had lost him again. 'Did you know?'

He said nothing, looked suddenly afraid, a small boy who had done something wrong.

She leaned forward, 'Please, Mr Best, please try and help me. Do you remember

160

that they had an affair?'

'Jean wasn't good for him.'

Jean? Yes, Jean, his first wife. 'And Eileen, was she good for him?'

'He loved his wife.'

'Helen or Jean?'

'Helen was lovely.'

'She's my mother.'

Mr Best looked at her now, something burned through the haze. 'Is she happy?'

'Yes.'

'She had to leave,' he said.

'Why?'

'It was because of the war. That's what I thought. He was in a camp, you see.'

She tried to keep her voice quiet, to steady his hand as they turned this corner of his mind.

'What was because of the war?'

But he left her. 'I said to Margaret, 'What a pity we didn't meet when we were young.' They are very careless here, you see, and she died when they operated.'

17

Baptist has a radio, a small, battery-operated wireless. Dr McMullen gave it to him one Christmas. On afternoons when Baptist has his off time he comes over to your house to sit with you and Rosa and talk and listen to the radio. He walks holding the radio up to his ear, and when he sits down on the old lawn chair behind the kitchen he carefully places it on the ground by his feet.

Mostly the Voice of Kenya plays African music, the tinny wahwah of voices and drums. For a while 'Kung Fu Fighting' is popular and you know the words by heart. Everybody does: it was so exciting, fast as lightning. Baptist doesn't approve. He says it isn't African music and the government station shouldn't play it. You don't tell him you like 'Kung Fu Fighting' better than the African music, which is a lot of wailing and often in a language other than Swahili or Kiluhya, so Baptist probably doesn't know what they are singing about either. When the radio broadcast is finished, the announcer says: 'Keep on keeping on' in English, or 'Maendeleo' in Swahili.

Rosa and Baptist talk in Kiluhya, but if Rosa's friend Alice comes by they speak in Swahili. Then you can understand them. Alice is from the coast, she is Giriyama, but she goes to the same church as Rosa and Baptist so they can be friends. You and Alice help Rosa fold the laundry, the big white sheets that fold corner to corner, like a dance, perfect squares, you and Rosa moving in together and then out. Or you just sit drawing pictures in the dirt and listen. Grown-ups always have a lot to talk about and if you are quiet and small they don't remember you.

Alice works down the road for Mrs Richards. She says Mr and Mrs Richards are always fighting and that sometimes Mr Richards hits Mrs Richards. She says, one day Mrs Richards took everything out of Mr Richards' cupboards and threw it outside into the garden. She poured paraffin on it and was going to burn it, but then Mr Richards came home and there was a lot of shouting. He pulled out some of her hair and she scratched his face with her red nails.

There are other stories. Alice tells of Wambui, who works for the Swiss family, and is always running away from the Bwana Swiss. He pinches her buttocks so hard she bruises, but she is afraid to say anything because then she will lose her job.

Alice says Jacob is a cook for the Americans in the big house. The memsahib is always yelling at him but then, later, she will give him money.

'Why?' Baptist wants to know.

Alice shrugs. 'For nothing.'

'Not for nothing,' Baptist says and snorts. His nostrils flare like a horse's and he laughs. 'For something!'

'Taratibu,' Rosa says, glancing at you.

But why? Why does the American lady give the cook money for nothing? And why does Rosa say 'Be careful'? All grown-ups speak this way, mzungu or African, not finishing their sentences, saying only half of something.

'For nothing.' Alice is definite.

'Who can understand them,' Baptist wonders. 'If you ask them for money, they tell you 'No.' If you don't ask for it they give it to you.'

One day, according to Baptist, there was a big fight between the doctor and Memsahib McMullen. The doctor had said they must send Nina back to England, she was very sick. The memsahib cried and shouted and said that she would go back to England with Nina. He told her she could do what she wanted. She said what she wanted was to have a child who wasn't sick. You just want to get rid of us, she said, you're throwing us out like garbage. Baptist was listening in the hallway outside their bedroom, with the sheepskin pads on his feet polishing the floor.

He says, after a while the doctor came to memsahib and said, Nina needs proper help and that's the end of it.

Rosa says, 'So in England they can make that child better?'

'Perhaps,' says Alice. 'If God wills.'

'How can it be that God wills the doctors in England to cure such a child and yet He does nothing for our children?' Baptist says.

'God's will is not for us to question.' Rosa looks at him like he should know this already. Rosa really loves God and Jesus. 'God knows what is best for each one of us.'

Another day. Baptist is crying, his radio is silent. Rosa is rubbing his shoulders, they are speaking in Kiluhya. His hands are balled into fists and he is pressing them into his eyes and then hitting them against the side of his head. You move to him and put your hand on his leg. 'Pole,' you say softly. Whatever it is you are sorry, so sorry. 'Pole sana.'

Suddenly he gasps and looks at you and says in English, 'She would not give me the money! Why not? Only three hundred shillings! Three hundred!' Then he stands and walks quickly away from you and Rosa, back through the hedge to the McMullens'. He has forgotten his radio. You pick it up and start after him. But Rosa says, 'Atcha yeye.' Leave him.

She takes the radio to give to him later. 'His child has died,' she says. 'He had malaria and Baptist had no money for the doctari. He asked memsahib McMullen for an advance, but she said no, he has taken too many advances, and now the child has died.'

'But Bwana McMullen is a doctor, he could have taken care of Baptist's child,' you say.

Rosa shakes her head, 'For why? For nothing? For money. He is a doctor for muzungus.'

You say, 'I will give Baptist the money.'

Rosa touches your hair with her hands. 'Ah, mtoto yangu, mtoto ya Mungu, asante. Baptist has no more children. God has taken them all to Him.'

You ask Mum about Baptist's dead children. She says, 'Oh, sweetheart, it's very sad, I know. But, you see, death doesn't mean the same thing to them. Because it happens so often, they have so many children, they don't let themselves feel the way we do. Baptist will have more children. You'll see.'

You see African children playing in the dust beside the road with dirty clothes and snot. You think they are not loved and how terribly sad that they are not loved. Maybe Africans do not love at all. But Rosa loves. She loves you. You know this because she combs your wet hair slowly so as not to pull the tangles. Her hand takes yours sometimes and you know the roughness of her palm and the warmth of it.

18

On 5 July 1969, John phoned Helen from the office and told her Tom Mboya had been assassinated outside a chemist's shop in the city centre. He said: 'Stay in the house, lock the doors.'

'What's going to happen?' She was scared, and thought about that night in Uganda, the hands and faces coming out of the night. She wanted John to come home.

'Maybe nothing. Probably nothing,' he said.

'When will you be coming home?'

'I don't know,' he said. 'Just stay in the house.'

As he was saying this, she was looking out the window. She saw Baptist coming through the hedge toward the kitchen, running with his radio. Helen ran downstairs. In the kitchen, Rosa was giving Ellie her lunch. Helen got there at the same time as Baptist. He was crying, speaking in Kiluhya to Rosa. Helen could only understand 'Tom Mboya, Tom Mboya.' The excitement frightened Ellie and she started crying. Rosa picked her up, rocking her on her hip, saying softly, 'Pole,

pole.' Rosa's eyes filled with tears and she looked at Helen.

'They have killed him.'

'I'm sorry,' Helen said, and in that moment, witnessing Rosa's sorrow, she foresaw what would happen, how the politicians would betray Rosa and Baptist and Sam and Pious. There would be more assassinations, there would be crackdowns and disappearances. Independence would become nothing more than a holiday day with parades and speeches.

There were police sirens in the street, and from the other direction, the sound of someone howling in grief.

Rosa looked at Helen. 'What will happen?'

Nothing, Helen thought, or everything. She realized how madness was always a moment away in Africa. Anger and bitterness, hunger and death waited patiently at the front gate. Rosa knew this essential state of helplessness, all Africans did. But we whites manage to convince ourselves that the order of our lives, the ironed clothes and the proper placement of cutlery, that these things can ward off disease or too much rain or too little or road accidents or assassinations. We're so surprised when things go wrong, so outraged.

'We must lock the doors,' Helen said. 'Get what you need from your room and bring it

169

back here quickly. Bring Pious and Sam.'

'It is a Kikuyu who has done this,' said Baptist.

'But Pious himself didn't do it,' Helen said. 'And you should be next door with Memsahib McMullen.'

But Eileen was at the door. She was holding Nina, her face white and stricken. 'They're going to kill us, these black bastards, they'll kill us all.'

Helen put an arm around Eileen, 'It's okay, sit down. You're safe.'

But Eileen was looking at Rosa and Baptist. 'What are they doing here? They'll kill us, they'll slash our throats.' She clutched little all-wrong Nina to her and screamed, 'Get them out! Get them out!'

Helen said, 'It's safer for them in here.'

'Safer for them? You're bloody mad to keep them in here!' Eileen shouted. 'It's safe for them in the bloody jungle.'

Helen turned to her, angry, 'Stop it!'

Rosa touched Helen's arm, 'It's better we go.' She handed Ellie back. Ellie cried and reached toward Rosa, but Rosa didn't turn, she walked quietly out with Baptist. Helen locked the door after them and thought about how often skin colour dictated action, how colour was the first thing one saw about a person. There seemed no way past that.

She went around the house, locking the doors and windows. Every window had bars built in to the stone, every door had a sliding grille. She'd never thought about the house as a fortress until now. Or how easily a fortress could become a prison. It was difficult to shut her mind to the possibilities: looting and killing. If the Africans turned against the whites, if all those years of being treated like dirt spun like a dust devil into a fine point of hate.

She grabbed a bottle of John's whisky and walked back to the kitchen. Ellie was crying, confused and frightened, mainly by Eileen who was taking knives out of the knife drawer and holding them up to the light. Nina, with her drifting eyes, was inert on her back on the floor. She was a rag-doll in beautiful clothes. In those early years, she never cried, she never made a sound.

'Sit down, Eileen,' Helen said, lifting Ellie into her arms. 'You're frightening the children.'

But Eileen had the knife sharpener out. 'We must be ready. We must fight them. It's not the rape I'm afraid of, not the physical act, but they have diseases.'

Helen grabbed her arm, roughly, and said, 'Sit down. This is my house and you'll do as I say. We're safe. I've locked everything.' She handed Eileen the whisky. 'Pour us both a glass.' And Eileen did.

They waited in the living room. The afternoon sun filtered in as always and the birds sang on. Ellie was playing quietly with her toys, Nina was asleep, and Eileen kept drinking. There was very little traffic noise, there was a dense stillness, and few people were out on the street. The charcoal seller and the fruit vendors would have gone somewhere, hidden somewhere.

The radio was turned to the BBC World Service. Tom Mboya's killer had been arrested. People were urged to go home peacefully, businesses were closing up in the downtown area.

Were there riots or angry mobs standing on corners? She wondered about Sam. Where was he? He had the capacity for trouble.

'Who the bloody hell is Tom bloody Boy anyway?' Eileen said.

'Tom Mboya,' Helen said. 'He's a politician, a respected one, more of a statesman. He's very popular here and internationally.'

'Respected? A munt? Then why'd they kill him?' Eileen sunk another glass. 'Why do they do anything? Ask an African why he picks his nose and he wouldn't have an effing clue.'

'Mboya was a Luo. Kenyatta is a Kikuyu. Maybe that has something to do with it, it's a

172

tribal power struggle. But I don't know that much about it.' I should, Helen thought, I should pay attention because there is so much at stake. But she was frightened, too; she could never know and understand this country, these people. She had no instinct and that made trust impossible.

'We should leave them to it, let them kill each other,' Eileen said. She looked out the window and the sun hit her face in such a way that Helen could see every line. Eileen's face was a road map of her disappointment. 'God I detest this country,' she said and reached for the whisky.

★ ★ ★

There were no riots that day or the next. Busloads of Luos and Luhyas arrived in town in anticipation of Mboya's funeral. Driving around, Helen saw clutches of them on the pavements. The men were sombre, talking amongst themselves, the women were often crying, sending up waves of ululations. She saw how everyone, men, women and children were picking up stones, quietly, and putting them in their pockets.

John had insisted there was nothing to be afraid of, he'd made her go out. 'It's not us they want,' he'd said. 'That's what you need

173

to understand. They're not interested in us, we just think they are because we're so arrogant, we believe we have to matter.' Then, pouring another glass, 'It's their history now.'

'What if something happens? A riot and I'm in the car?'

'What if you're in England and there's a riot? There are plenty of them at the moment.'

'This isn't England. And if it was I wouldn't be in a city where there are riots.'

'They'll go for each other first and then the Asians. We're way down on the list.'

'I'm just afraid.'

'Of what?' He had lost his patience. 'We've got passports and money. We can leave when we need to. England, Scotland, Australia. The poor bloody watu are stuck here.'

What should I do about Ellie, she'd wanted to ask him. Do I leave her with Rosa as usual when I go out, as if nothing has happened, no good man has been assassinated, no future for millions ruined — even if they don't know it yet? Do I trust my child to someone I threw out of my house only days ago for fear of having my throat cut? Or do I bring my child with me in the car and take the chance that things don't turn violent? She thought of cars immolating on city streets, of bricks sailing through the air. She thought of Prague, of

Vietnam. The world was coming undone.

And here was the real reason for her foray into a city trembling on the edge of violence: John's whisky supply was running low. For a moment, Helen envied Eileen's weakness, how she was allowed to collapse in a foam of green chiffon on her bed, summoning Baptist for tea and boiled eggs, demanding, ordering, chastising. She had sent a shopping list over to Helen in the morning and then phoned with specific instructions. 'The mountain pawpaws, *not* the ones from the coast. And make sure the butcher trims the fat.' All this without even asking. Just assuming. Bloody hell. Assuming that Baptist wouldn't quit because he couldn't no matter how much she abused him. He needed the job.

But how could you ever envy Eileen with her half-child?

Helen did as she was told. She strapped Ellie into the front seat, she pretended not to notice Rosa's hurt look, the one that said, I have done nothing to deserve this. She drove to the dukhas and bought Eileen's damn mountain pawpaws and collected John's whisky and the dry cleaning.

On the way home, driving down Uhuru Highway, she saw clouds of smoke over downtown. A mile later she realized it wasn't smoke but tear gas. Even at this distance it stung her eyes and throat. She pulled over and found a handkerchief in her handbag and tied it around Ellie's face.

'Mummy, why do my eyes hurt?'

'It's the air, sweetheart, something in the air. We'll be home soon and it'll be better there.'

★ ★ ★

On the day of Mboya's funeral Sam didn't show up for work. Helen knew he wouldn't, but she'd hoped he'd at least ask her for the day off; she'd have given it to him. He hadn't said a word all week. He'd done his work, chopping and cooking, moving about the kitchen like a black hole, his anger sucking in the air and light around him. At first Helen was afraid of him, but then she saw that John was right, Sam didn't care about her or any of the whites.

She was reading about the Mau Mau. One hundred whites died, many of them soldiers. The way everyone talked about it you'd think it had been a wholesale slaughter of the innocents. Oh, and as a footnote: 13,500 Africans had died, 30,000 were interred without trial in camps where beatings and forced labour were the norm. Our soldiers, Helen thought, our lily-white policemen and our District Commissioners, those good, hearty souls, those heroes defending the Crown, who drink at the Muthaiga Club and know what's best for the Africans, they beat 30,000 Africans and imprisoned them and called any desire they expressed for independence, for self-determination, *a threat to national security.*

But what did she know? She was just a housewife with her nice, sybaritic life, her rich husband. What she thought and what she knew and what she spoke about at dinner and cocktail parties were all different things. She hid her opinions the way she hid whisky bottles.

Helen sat in the living room and listened to the World Service as Rosa and Baptist sat listening to VoK behind the kitchen. The police had fired tear gas into the cathedral where the funeral was held. There were riots, thousands of people running up Kenyatta Avenue, trampling the flowerbeds, the agapanthus and the lilies, and smashing shop windows. But in the end the crowds were dispelled. The centre of Nairobi was cordoned off, leaving the crowds nowhere to gather. The still, empty streets, ghosting with tear gas, were littered with thousands of shoes, flip-flops or cheap plastic shoes without laces or flapping old leather sandals, hand-me-downs from white bwanas, shoes that fell off when you ran, or that you discarded because you weren't used to shoes and it was easier to run away on bare feet.

19

At last Ellie could see the lake, a silver sequin pinned to the vast bleached floor of the Rift Valley, an hour away. She was driving along the escarpment that edged the Rift, a notoriously dangerous road. The woman at the car rental agency had been concerned.

'You are alone?'

'Yes.'

'It is not good to drive alone.'

'Well, I am alone. I will be careful.'

'You must not drive at night, the road is very bad and there are bad people.'

Despite her concern, the woman had taken Ellie's credit card and handed over the keys.

The night hid all demons, but in the day you could see the danger and how the woods that once covered these highlands had been cut down for smallholdings of beans and stumpy corn. The road was a connection of potholes, lined by broken-down vehicles. What did move moved fast. Ancient buses coughed like tubercular patients, but their condition belied the light-speed they attained as they raced big semis hauling UN grain or cows on the straight-aways. Decrepit Toyota pickups loaded with Africans and goats overtook on blind curves.

As she slowed down to avoid a donkey in the middle of the road, a black Mercedes with tinted windows floored it past her. This wasn't driving but surviving, a mad, high-speed jockeying for tarmac and life. Every day the buses crashed, the trucks sailed over the escarpment and burst into flame, bodies strewn like laundry on a windy day. Mothers, sisters, brothers.

But no matter. Death doesn't mean the same thing to them.

How do we know? Ellie wondered. Did we ever ask?

On the roadside small boys held rabbits by the ears and waved them at oncoming traffic. Thin men sold boxes of plums. They were overeager in their torn shirts. She wanted to buy the rabbits, but what the hell was she going to do with a carload of rabbits? So she bought more plums than she could possibly eat.

For a moment she stood by her car, eating a plum and staring into the Rift that fell away at her feet. Here, the continent had tried to sub-divide itself millions of years ago. One day it would succeed and the sea would come rushing onto the plains below, the salt air would lift up, the sea spray would wash away all traces of humankind's sad, dusty existence on the valley's sharp rim. But now, a thousand feet below her, there remained the dip and sweep of earth toward a far horizon where the planet collided with the sky. Between here and there, a few roads scratched the dust, going somewhere, she supposed, but there seemed no destination, just some human scrabbling for direction. The volcano, Longonot, rose like a barnacle from the dry plains, and the listening station's white dishes gazed skyward. As a child Ellie had wondered what they were listening for. God, perhaps, awaiting further instructions, like Moses on Sinai. But God said very little.

Beyond was the lake, blinking in the sun.

The road started downward, a steep descent that crabbed along the escarpment in a series of perilous curves. Halfway down, tucked into a narrow canyon of rock was a tiny church built by the Italian prisoners of war whose forced labour was responsible for the road. Ellie parked and walked up the rough-hewn steps. A cold wind spiralled up from the Rift and pulled her hair loose. She had always loved this church and the humility of the men who built it. They knew how little they mattered in this vast landscape, how the wind could carry them off or the earth swallow them. Inside the vestry, someone had placed fresh wildflowers in a tin vase on the altar.

Ellie sat on one of the three pews. The air was cold and she shivered. There was the smell of brass polish and candle wax. The last time she had sat here she had believed in God. She had believed He lived in the Rift Valley. It was the only place big enough for Him, because she had known that much about God: He was everywhere so He was very big. Her faith had been Rosa's faith, an extension of her love for Rosa. God made Rosa happy so God must be good. But true faith requires a stubbornness that Ellie couldn't muster even then. How could God exist and let Idi Amin smash people to death with pangas under the mango trees? How could God let all Baptist's children die? How could you live in Africa and believe in God? The land, staggeringly beautiful, is indifferent, the seasons do as they want, the bad men always get away. We left the dark forest for the light of the open plains six million years ago, Ellie thought, but the darkness followed us, and entered us. Maybe it was always in us, the loamy soil in which our hearts grow.

She left the church and drove on. As the road levelled out, the horizon tilted and the lake disappeared. She approached it from another dimension now, as a line of green trees ten miles ahead. The town came out to meet her, one or two roadside bars, a Quonset hut, an old man with a stream of cows, and then a gathering of shanties, dozens of goats, chickens, children selling peanuts and roasted mealies.

Soon, she was in the midst of crumbling colonial-era buildings and a dozen cement-block hotels: The Paradise Bar and Hotel, The Green Satellite Inn. Dust devils and donkeys roamed at will. Condom ads covered billboards and buildings. 'Sema nami' — Talk to me, they said. Talk to me about AIDS and love and dying, the new trinity of intimacy in Africa. The town's residents, many of whom, if the statistics were right, would die of AIDS, watched her drive past.

Two miles on, she turned at the sign into a canopy of yellow fever trees. The hotel's low buildings were whitewashed and red-roofed, the doorway arched by roses. Inside, it was gloomy and smelled of wood polish and cabbage. The floors creaked. It was an old hotel, once popular with settlers and whites weekending from Nairobi, and had the atmosphere of a museum — though she felt nothing had been purposely preserved; rather, no one had thought to change or even move the red leather couches crowded around the fireplace, the worn zebra skins and sheepskin rugs. The doors opened onto a wide veranda and the green lawn rolled down to the blue lake.

An old man carried her bag to a cottage. The water was a paler blue from this angle but the lake smell was strong: reeds, dark, sucking mud, saltless tides. The old man said the level of the lake was dropping, it used to come all the way to here and now you can see the papyrus is in the middle not at the edge. The golf courses and the flower farms around the lake were taking too much water, he said. The flowers were flown out every night to Holland.

His children worked at the farms so the farms were good. He didn't really understand the flowers, why people in Europe wanted them so much. After all, you couldn't eat them. Ellie said it was because of the rain and the grey skies, people needed flowers because there was so little sun. He wanted to know how much the flowers cost to buy there, in Europe. Ellie told him about three thousand shillings for a dozen roses. He didn't believe her — this was his monthly wage.

When he left, she sat in a camp chair on the grass in front of the cottage. There were water-skiers out on the lake, the drone of their boat looping back and forth. Rich whites from Nairobi with powerboats and time on their hands. Closer, she heard starlings, a hoopoe, the guests in the next cottage talking in low voices. If Peter was here they might have made love in the lumpy, creaking bed, or they might also have talked in low voices and laughed softly together. But he was tucked away, far away in his own life. He was looking over blueprints, measuring countertops, trying to seduce the cat.

★   ★   ★

At dinner, the other guests were parcelled off — an old white Kenyan couple, three African businessmen, six American Peace Corps workers — eating the over-cooked roast beef or the Shepherd's Pie. No one looked up or smiled in greeting. Alone, it was possible to slip through hotels and towns, unnoticed. It was possible to slip through life untarnished.

★   ★   ★

The next morning she drove to the Naivasha police station. The staff sergeant rose to meet her and took off his hat. She explained that she was hoping to get hold of some police records from 1960, perhaps she could read the incident report book. His uniform was pressed and clean. He wanted to help but he

185

said there were no records and no report book from then because of a fire ten years ago.

In general, he didn't care for mzungus. They were rude when he pulled them over for speeding or other traffic violations. They behaved as if the law was not for them. Not all of them were like this, but most of them. However, they all eventually paid him what he asked for, pretending it was an on-the-spot fine and not a bribe that he would take and pay for his son's private education or to re-roof his house.

He asked her why she wanted these things.

She told him she believed her father had murdered a woman in 1974. In a file in Nairobi's CID she had found a notation that said 'Naivasha — July 6, 1960'. There was a murder recorded in Naivasha on that date, but the file was missing.

At first he thought he wouldn't help her. What did he care, some woman coming here with a piece of paper and some old story. But he noticed how careful she was, how she stood to one side. She did not demand.

He said: 'My father was a policeman here during those days. He's mzee now. But he might remember, if there was something to remember about that day.'

His father was at home now, he offered to

take her. They drove in the police car, which had been donated by the Danish government but was maintained by no one. Ellie noticed how the sergeant pumped the brakes in order to stop. The speedometer did not work, and there was no radio, only a gaping hole and loose wires as if it had been stolen. Even so, the car's interior was clean. The sergeant had standards, though the sliding scale of them was dragged ever downward by the corruption and mismanagement of his superiors.

The old man was sitting on a stool in the shade of a yellow-barked acacia, leaning on his walking stick. Despite the heat of the midday he was wearing a tweed cap and a heavy wool jacket. Behind him was a neat cinder-block house painted a jaunty blue. Women were sorting beans on gunnysacks spread out in the dirt. Children skipped rope and raced toy cars made from tin cans and wire.

'This is my father, Captain Muthengi,' said the sergeant. The old man stood, but was so stooped that standing he was no taller than he had been sitting. He was shaped like a question mark. He shook her hand, looking up at her. The pupils of his eyes were rimmed with grey.

'She wants to ask you about an incident

that happened in 1960, on July sixth,' the sergeant said.

Captain Muthengi smiled, '1960? Jack Robertson was our captain. Oh, we had discipline! Spit-shine on our boots, yes sir!' He snapped his heels together. 'I was strong then. And quick. Not like now, not like now.' His English was effortless.

A chair came for Ellie and a woman brought a tray of warm sodas, a package of sugar-encrusted biscuits. All this sugar, she realized, it's cheap energy for an insufficient diet. And it's a small treat, a small luxury.

'1960. What can I tell you? My memory is not so good.'

Ellie drank a Fanta. 'John Cameron. Do you remember his name? Or Eileen McMullen?'

The old man thought about it and shook his head. 'I'm sorry.'

'It's too long ago,' she said.

He tilted his head. 'But there was something. Maybe it was 1960 or '61. It was before Independence, maybe two or three years. A woman was killed. A white woman. Yes, maybe 1960, maybe at the end of the rains.'

Ellie waited.

'She was killed. On her farm, out near where you find Kongoni Farm now. The

188

workers found her in the grass. The grass was long, so, yes, after the rains. Yes, it might be July. But the date? It is not possible.'

He held up his hand, smiling. Each memory was a small victory for him now. 'Yes, yes. It was a big shida, a memsahib dead. She was married. Her husband was a hunter, always away on safari. Bwana Bunduki they called him because he loved guns. Not just for hunting, but for shooting, sometimes shooting at people, but never hitting them, just for macheza, for a game. The watu said she had many boyfriends. Who knows. Maybe one of them, maybe her husband. But there was no proof, no evidence — and you cannot just arrest a mzungu and hope he tells you, 'Yes, I did this thing'. But she was not so good, this woman, I remember. At the time I thought maybe her servants, the cook or the shamba boy killed her. She was always abusing them. Anyway, we arrested some young men, they were troublemakers, maybe they had been Mau Mau. They were just jambazi, you know, thugs. We arrested them and charged them. They went to prison up there past Nakuru.'

'Do you think it was them?' Ellie asked.

But Muthengi shrugged. 'If not them they did something bad anyway.'

'Do you remember the names, Bwana

Bunduki's real name?'

After a while he shook his head. 'They were friends of Robertson. All wazungu knew each other then. Their names? No. Something maybe German, not English, not Smith or Lewis. I'm trying to remember but not English. She was not thin or fat like English women. She was . . . full, like an African bibi. Mapendeza, you understand? The way she looked was trouble for men. I saw her sometimes driving along the road here, driving very fast, she didn't care if maybe she hit someone or this old mama carrying firewood falls into the ditch. 1960, July, someone killed her. Yes.'

The sergeant looked at Ellie: 'I know the place, on the other side of the lake.'

'Can you tell me how to get there?'

'It is better I take you.'

Old Muthengi said, 'Why do you want to know this?'

'Her father killed a woman. She thinks there is some connection,' said the sergeant.

'Connection, how?' the old man asked.

Ellie felt sweat in her palms. 'I don't know. It was just a note in an old police file. I don't know what this woman had to do with my father. Maybe its not even the right date.' But she didn't believe that. And Muthengi saw her lie.

He shook his head. 'You must honour your father. You must not think these things of him.'

'How can I honour him?' she said. 'My father was not a good man.'

He held up his finger. 'It was the watu who killed her.' His voice was stern and definite, and she could imagine the proud, certain young policeman he had once been.

But his son said, 'The wazungu could do as they wanted in those days.'

His father said something to him in Kikuyu, a sharp rebuke. The sergeant looked away, chastened, and gave no reply.

★ ★ ★

As they drove away, the sergeant told her what the old man had said. ' 'In those days things were better.' ' He laughed briefly, 'Oh, yes indeed, my father was a proud servant of your Queen. And Jack Robertson was a hero. Jack Robertson, we knew him as 'Kiboko' because he always carried a whip. You know kiboko is hippo and also whip in Swahili. Kiboko, he liked his name very much.'

'What happened to him?'

'He died. After independence, from some illness, I don't know, a heart attack. But everyone here said the mganga had put a spell on him and killed him.'

'Do you believe that?'

He laughed again, 'I am a Christian. I do not believe in the mganga.' And then he repeated his father's words in Kikuyu, angry and laughing at the same time.

★ ★ ★

They rounded the lake on the rutted, dusty road. The extraordinary beauty of the landscape had resisted the drought, the giant fig trees and groves of yellow-barked acacias, the steep dry hillsides and the blue lake rimmed with green. Once, her parents had spoken of moving here, of buying a small farm. She had been promised a pony. She tried to imagine them, bound in the intimacy of a shared dream. In her memory they moved around each other, away from each other, mute as mannequins. Had they touched and murmured and looked out across this lake, believing there was a chance for them after all?

'Here, this place,' said the sergeant, turning right and across a cattle guard. He drove on for a few hundred yards until the track ran out in the long, dry grass. They got out of the car and as they walked grasshoppers leapt away from their feet. High above, an Augur buzzard surfed the hot wind. Ellie wondered if life could have been different, if this wide and living land could have changed her father, somehow dislodged the darkness, drawn it out of him like a splinter. She wondered, too, how the death that had happened here connected to Eileen's death, and so to her father.

And why she wanted it to.

The silence surrounded them for miles in every direction. Ellie felt you could walk for hours and hear nothing but low wind and cicadas. She thought about the dead woman, how this was the last of the world she had seen, this same silence between her and anyone who might save her.

Then, from a path along the lake, came two old women carrying firewood on their backs. The sergeant went down toward them, spoke to them. He glanced back at her, gestured for her. She walked to him.

'These women live in a village near here,' he said. 'They say they remember when the woman died because the police came to their village and asked many questions.'

'Did they know her, the woman?' Ellie looked at the old faces. Their lives had been shaped by burden: carrying firewood, carrying water, carrying children. They must be in their seventies now and they'll be carrying their coffins to their graves, she thought.

One woman spoke in Kikuyu, the sergeant translated. 'She only knew her driving past or on her horse.'

'Does she know who killed her?'

No, the woman didn't. She believed it was Mau Mau, some men from Mau Mau. The ones who were arrested were known in the area for stealing and even killing. Then she said some other mzungu had come asking these same questions. After the woman had died but before Moi became President, before 1979. A man, a policeman from Nairobi, fat and with red hair.

He had written the note, it must be him, and he had come here, he had believed there was a connection.

'Patrick O'Shea,' Ellie said.

The sergeant looked at her, 'You know this man?'

No, she told him.

But she remembered him taking Baptist away and Rosa's fear and her tears.

'Do you know him?'

'When I was beginning with the police, he was still working. I did not meet him. But they said about him that he took certain prisoners into the woods and shot them. He was like Kiboko, only stronger. The watu, they were afraid of him, very afraid.'

'And now? Where is he now?'

The sergeant smiled, 'You know, one day I came home and found my father wearing his best suit, the one he keeps for weddings or christenings. I asked him why he was wearing this and he said, 'Because today the Devil has died and I am going to celebrate.' '

★ ★ ★

They drove back. When they reached the police station, a young man was waiting. He handed Ellie an envelope.

'Mzee Muthengi sent this for you.'

The envelope was so recently stuck that the glue was moist. On a piece of paper torn from a spiral notebook was written, in shaky ballpoint pen:

RIKTOF

A name. It must be their name, the dead woman and her husband, the hunter.

20

Mrs McMullen is holding your father's sweater. He is trying to turn away, his face is already turned away, but she holds on to the red sweater.

'John, please,' she says. Her lipstick has smudged above her mouth.

Your legs are beginning to get cramps, little knots in your knees. You stretch out one leg and then the other, very slowly, not rustling the leaves. Just this small corner of the window but you can see the whole room inside, Nina's room, but without Nina now.

'Don't,' he says, trying to get her hands off him.

But she clings tighter, now with her body against his. 'John, I love you.'

She is married to Dr McMullen but she loves your father. He doesn't love her. He pulls away from her and she grabs him, his arm, and then he pulls that away from her. He is walking toward the door. She gets down on her knees.

'I'll do anything, please, anything.'

He opens the door.

She throws her arms around his legs.

'Let me go, Eileen,' he says.

She won't, she presses her cheek against his legs, holding tight.

'I want to have your child.'

She won't let go.

He raises his voice, 'Goddammit!'

'A baby, our baby,' she says.

He tries to walk but she is around his legs. They are stuck together, a three-legged race.

He reaches down and grabs at her hands, trying to pull them away but she sticks to him. So he pulls her hair. She won't let go. He kicks out at her and she falls back on the floor. In the second he turns again for the door she comes at him, this time with her nails. She scratches at him. She shouts: 'I love you!'

He hits out at her but she doesn't care, she keeps snatching at him, she is trying to catch pieces of him like a monkey stealing pawpaws from the tree. He hits her properly and she spins away from him.

'Please, Eileen!' he shouts back at her.

Mrs McMullen looks up at him, she has fallen against the bed and Nina's stuffed toys. 'I'll tell her,' she says, 'I'll tell her everything. She doesn't love you, she doesn't love you — '

Then he makes her be quiet. He pushes her down on the bed and puts his hand over her face. 'Shut up,' he says, not shouting now but in his low warning voice. 'Shut up.' She moves under him, but you see that she is not trying to move away from him but to him, pressing his hand even harder against her face. 'Touch me, touch me.'

Your father stands quickly and pushes his hand through his hair, and then he walks from the room. Mrs McMullen says, 'It's me you want, it's me you want.' But your father is gone, he is not hearing, he is already out of the house and walking back across the lawn, through the hedge.

21

John's mother, Agnes, gave Helen an envelope containing his childhood pictures. She said to Helen, 'I can't keep everything and I know if I give these to John he'll just put them away somewhere and they'll never see the light of day.'

The collection covered the first five years of her husband's life. It began with him as a baby in the arms of an African in a white uniform and ended with him and Agnes on the dock in Dar es Salaam: John, aged four, leaving for school in Scotland, Agnes saying goodbye, the ship behind them, the sea and the palm trees. It struck Helen that this was indeed the entire extent of John's childhood — and Agnes's motherhood.

Agnes had come to visit, as she did every few years. Helen liked her, she was an easy guest, an undemanding mother-in-law, an elegant old lady who dressed carefully and never left the house without a hat. She lived alone in a large flat in Inverness. She had taught violin until arthritis bent her fingers and swelled her knuckles. She read Robert Louis Stevenson and Daniel Defoe; she didn't approve of modern authors. To Helen she seemed utterly self-contained. Agnes expected nothing, no tributes, no affection. In turn she was detached, she gave nothing back. She had clearly drawn a boundary between herself and the rest of the world.

For the world had stripped Agnes of the men she loved, one by one. Her husband had died of cancer in the forties and she had never remarried. Her beloved brothers had both died in the Great War. And John, she had sent away, she had given away.

'Let's have a tipple,' she said to Helen. They were alone, John was at the office, Ellie at school. It was after lunch. Several tipples later, she brought out the photograph.

The brandy made Agnes bold, she wanted Helen to know about John, to try and understand him. She was wise enough, and experienced enough, to know that sympathy was what you resorted to when love and respect had packed their bags and moved out. Sympathy had saved marriages before.

Agnes, as the wife of a civil servant in the early days of the Tanganyika colony, had done what was expected, attended the cocktail parties, trained the servants to starch collars and roast lamb, and put her child on a boat and sent him to school back home. There, he would be educated so that he would grow up to obtain a respectable job, to be a gentleman, not the kind of wild child one occasioned to see on the up-country farms. Agnes saw her son every two years, sometimes every three when she herself went back to Scotland on leave. She put John on the HMS *Dunluce Castle* in 1928, when he was four years old.

She remembered the day, very clearly, when she packed her only son's little shirts and his little socks into a little suitcase. She didn't let him take his favourite blankie or bunny because he had to be a little man now. She didn't cry when she walked him up the gangway and he didn't cry either. He didn't cling to her or waver, he walked on straight and brave. Like a little man. She didn't think about the next time she'd see him, when he would be five inches taller, his cheeks would not be so round, that he would be a stranger, someone else's child, the school's child, not hers, or not a child at all.

Goodbye, little man, goodbye my little man, Agnes said, being brave enough for both of them because tears were forbidden. All the other mothers were there with their little boys. The little boys were lined up on deck waving back down at the mothers. Not smiling, not crying, already learning to lock away what they felt. If they cried they would be teased: baby, baby.

The mothers were lined up along the dock, not crying but smiling because they'd had so much practice at pretend smiles. The sea was bright, dazzling blue; the thick, briny air soaked linen dresses to the spine. And in vagrant currents came the sea-salt smell of engine oil and dried fish. The Africans were carrying cargo, sacks of sugar and flour. Sailors ran and loosened ropes and made others fast. All this movement and yet Agnes's heart was dead still. A stopped clock. It would never move again.

The mothers were waving as the ship blew its horn and pulled away from the dock. Waving until it was time to go home and organize the next drinks party. Waving and then going home and shutting the doors to their little boys' rooms.

Looking at the picture — John stands straight, shoulders back, as he imagines a soldier must stand, but instead he looks like a thin boy trying to fit through a narrow space frontward — Helen thought that the ship's stewards might as well have thrown him overboard then and there, he'd have drowned in salt water instead of whisky.

She knew Agnes was well-meaning, that she wanted her son to be happy and well. Agnes's feelings for John were tangled with guilt and remorse and grief. Agnes had to live with that day on the docks and how the details of it grew sharper over the years instead of dimmer. She knew what she'd done and saw the consequences; she was not blind to the drinking.

'He loves you,' Agnes said.

Helen almost laughed. She'd tried that one, love being a trap and a weapon and a threat. She'd said to John: 'If you love me you'll stop drinking.' When that failed, she threatened, 'I'll leave if you don't stop drinking.' It took her a long time to understand that she was asking him to make a choice he didn't have to make. He could have her and keep on drinking. He already knew what she had yet to find out: that she couldn't leave. Without money, without a plane ticket, without the strength for leaving. And a child to be fed and clothed.

Still, Helen had hope. She could still see their way clear of the whisky. The old dream held fast. The memory of love was hard to distinguish from the actual presence, or absence, of love: John had lifted her free from the car, he'd banished her death, he'd sent it scurrying into the Ugandan bush. He was her hero. She was determined to believe what she had believed then.

But if I'd known about this photograph,

would I have married him, she wondered. Knowing what I know now, would I have been able to decline love when it came — that great force upon my heart? Wise enough? I didn't have a choice because I didn't know. I thought love was all that mattered.

If Agnes had known what would happen to her son, would she have put him on that ship? Would she have been brave enough to flout protocol, her husband, and the entire mindset that determined boys must go to school in the cold north and wear pressed charcoal wool shorts and pulled-up socks, they must learn Latin and pour the milk *after* the tea? They must on no account run brown-skinned and skinned-kneed, all tawny-gold and liquid motion, like sunlight on sea.

Perhaps it was wrong to burden one day with so much. Other children had made the same journey and survived those cruel, cold schools. Maybe if there hadn't also been the war and the blue Pacific and the men below waiting for him to fall. Maybe if Helen herself had been a different person, if she weren't so naïve and silly. And maybe if everything could be different then apples might also fall upwards.

She was finding bottles all the time now. She reckoned he was drinking one a day. But only in the evenings and at parties. At the office he was perfectly sober, his shirts ironed and hair combed back, his mathematician's brain snapping through columns of figures. His drink at lunchtime lasted him all day — unless there was a bottle hidden in his office.

In the evening, here was her choice: to stay in and watch him drink in his chair in the corner, their conversation trickling into a silence as dense and immovable as granite. Or to go out to dinners and cocktail parties and see him laugh and joke, to have him put his arm around her and kiss her affectionately, and then the terrifying drive home, veering through the dark, objects rushing into the headlights. Either way, the evenings ended the same: she helped him up the stairs, she helped him out of his clothes.

'He loves you,' Agnes said.

Love is also an oath and a promise. It's a point of honour, an act of courage. Helen knew she was being asked to be strong enough to love enough, or maybe just strong enough to stay, because she wasn't strong enough to leave. She knew if she left the failure of the marriage would be her failure, her fault. And without her marriage, who would she be? What would she have to show for herself?

22

Ellie had the piece of paper in her pocket. She was driving, thinking about the name and the named, imagining them. The woman with her dyed blonde hair and over-plucked eyebrows, her hard blue eyes and her cigarettes. Hating Africa, the dirty, thieving Africans, the dust, the mud, but hating Germany more. In Germany she would have been a mere mortal, a middle-class girl destined to marry a restaurant owner who stank of cooked meat and sauerkraut. But in Africa, she was dangerous and slinky, she had money, cowering servants, a huge house overlooking the lake. She didn't even have to draw her own bathwater, she left her dirty underpants on the floor for someone else to clean. But like so many others, she'd forgotten that she was not special, just white.

And Bwana Bunduki, polishing his guns by the fire, his heart an abattoir of animals. Lion, rhino, elephant, leopard, buffalo all bowed down and fell at his feet. They gave their lives for his glory. He was a tough, sun-hardened man, Africa was his stage, the garden where he was master and lord.

Ellie saw the woman's body in the long grass, hidden in lush green fragrant grass, a leopard-print scarf around her neck. The vultures had found it first. That's how you found any body in Africa, you looked for the circling of vultures, their death reel in the sky.

★　★　★

'Mr Harrison?'

'Speaking.'

'This is Eleanor Cameron, John Cameron's daughter.'

'Yes?' He was trying to put it together, maybe he'd forgotten that John Cameron had once had a family. 'Oh, yes.' More confident now. 'I'm so sorry about your father. We're all going down like nine-pins, the old guard.'

'Mr Harrison, that's why I've called. I wondered if I could talk to you about him.'

'Call me Berry, for God's sake. Only person calls me Mr Harrison is the Indian chap who owns the dukha. I'm afraid we'd rather lost touch, your father and I.'

'It's really about before. Before we left. The early seventies.'

'I can't promise much — ' A manic barking interrupted him. He put his hand over the receiver, 'Shut up, you stupid mutts!' And then, 'My wife's dogs. Absolutely useless but

207

they mean the world to her. Well, why don't you come to lunch, tomorrow? Would that suit you? Come early and we can talk before the other guests come. About noon? Have you got a pencil? I'll give you directions.'

★   ★   ★

Ruth and Berry Harrison lived in Langata. Here were big houses with big gardens, vanloads of security guards parked on strategic corners. The logo on the vans warned of an 'ARMED RESPONSE'. The Maasai were here as well, with their reedy, twitching cattle, grazing on the dusty verges, staring over fences at green lawns and swimming pools.

On the Harrisons' gate a sign: 'HAKUNA KAZI. MBWA KALI SANA!' There is no work. The dogs are very fierce. The same words had hung on the gates to the Kitisuru house. Except one day the gates had been open, or perhaps the man hadn't been able to read the sign, and he'd come around to the kitchen. Ellie remembered his shoes worn through at the toes, the rags masquerading as a suit, but shirt still buttoned to the neck. 'Kazi,' he said. 'Naomba.' Work, I beg you. He offered to clean up the dog shit on the lawn but Sam sent him away. And as he was walking back down the driveway the dogs gave chase, barking and snapping as the man ran back to the street. Chasing Africans, a marvellous game for white people's dogs.

The guard in his navy uniform with red piping opened the Harrisons' gate. Ellie drove up the long, gravelled driveway to a large graceful house overhung with golden shower and bougainvillea. A tide of Jack Russells poured out of the front door, spinning and yapping. In their wake came Ruth Harrison. For all her gracious living, she had not aged well. Her English beauty had dried in the African sun. Her skin, perma-tanned, was mottled as a lizard's. Across her lips, a slash of bright red.

'Hello!' she said.

Berry was the opposite of Ruth: pale, bald, portly. In another form Berry might have been a drunk or a buffoon, but he had a quick appraising stare. Ellie felt him scanning her. 'I can see your father in you, the chin, and you're tall like him.'

'Come in, come in, delighted you could come,' said Ruth.

'What will you drink?' said Berry.

They walked through the house with its chintz couches and velvet pillows. Animal heads stared down from the walls between old English landscape oils and exquisite watercolours of the East African coast. There were Yemeni daggers and Yoruba shields, Ethiopian crosses, ebony carvings from the Congo. It struck Ellie as the loot of conquerors. But no, Berry and Ruth were hardly that. Every window and door was braced with heavy steel security bars, there were panic buttons in every room.

Ruth led Ellie onto the veranda, Berry handed her a gin and tonic. Across the lawn, beyond the acacias and the swimming pool, the Ngongs rippled against a blue sky. Two warthogs nuzzled the grass. A second security guard patrolled with a German Shepherd.

Ruth saw her looking. 'Sundays have been the worst. It happened just up the road a month ago. They came in with guns and pangas. Sandy Wilson, his wife and baby. They killed them. Took what they could carry, the telly, the VCR.'

Berry Harrison took a sip of his drink, his eyes in the distance. 'Savages.'

'Do you ever think of leaving?' Ellie said.

'God, no,' Berry said. 'This is our home. It's difficult but there have been difficult times before. We're just careful.'

Ruth said, 'And we can't leave, really, anyway. We're both Kenyan citizens, we need visas just to visit England. Even if we wanted to we couldn't move there without standing in line with every Pakistani and Nigerian who wants to do the same thing.'

'Australia, America, it's the same thing. We're too old. Born here and die here, won't we, darling?' Berry lifted his drink to toast the hills.

Ruth turned to Ellie with a practised smile, 'And your mother, Helen, how is she?'

'Married that American chap, one from the bank, isn't that right?' said Berry.

'Yes, Gus Farrell. They're very happy. They live in Maine now.'

'How nice,' said Ruth. 'She was a lovely woman, your mother. We never met Gus.'

'I don't really know what we can tell you about John.' Berry had already finished his gin and tonic. He jiggled the glass so the ice cubes clinked and called out: 'Daniel!'

Daniel appeared, a slim African in a dark green cotton uniform. He had another drink all ready for the bwana.

'You were friends,' Ellie said.

'At the Club mostly. That was where we met, played golf, that sort of thing. And my firm used Cameron & Best.'

'I've been told he was a good accountant.'

'Oh, the best. Sharp as a knife. Never missed a trick.'

Ellie wondered how much of Berry's money her father had smuggled out of the country. Enough to buy a resident's visa in Gibraltar or Malta if it was needed. 'I don't remember him as a very happy man,' she said.

Berry shrugged. 'The marriage was difficult. He wasn't a man given to affection and I think your mother needed more. Most women do.'

Ruth gave a half-smile, 'Well, that's what we saw, dear.'

'I know he drank,' Ellie said.

'We all drank, John no more than most,' said Berry. But Ellie saw Ruth's gaze slip inadvertently to the drink in her husband's hand. 'No more than most' was a hell of a lot.

Ellie held her own glass in her lap. If she asked the wrong questions she would lose Berry. She kept her voice soft, free of insinuation.

'Did he know the Riktofs?'

'Riktoffen,' Ruth corrected. 'Goodness. Now, I haven't thought of them for years.'

'Maria and Nels,' said Berry.

'She died, didn't she?' Ruth was remembering. 'It was a long time ago.'

Berry said, 'Some Mau Mau business.'

'Was it?' Ellie said carefully.

'If not Mau Mau then some African. Theft or something.'

'I heard she was having an affair.'

'She had plenty of them.' Berry looked at her.

Ruth's lips pressed to a knife-edge.

'There was speculation that it was her lover or maybe her husband who killed her,' Ellie said.

'Speculation? No, merely gossip.' Berry raised his eyebrows. 'It wasn't Nels because he would have killed them both.'

'And her lover?'

Berry's eyes staying on her.

'Now I see where you're going with this.'

But Ellie didn't quite see.

And then she did.

This was where her thoughts had been leading, she knew now, like a thread through the Minotaur's caves. The conclusion lay before her, a body in the long green grass under a grey sky.

Berry leaned back. 'What do you want to know?'

'When?'

'Early sixties. Before your mother. Before independence. It must have been.'

'She died in 1960,' Ellie said.

'That's right. Yes.'

'Was he involved with her when — '

'He was in the Club — Muthaiga — when the news of her death came in. So was I. That's why I remember. We all bought him drinks. We all knew about the affair. Except Nels.'

'Is Nels still alive?'

'God, no. Gored by a buffalo up in Narok a long time ago.' Berry didn't hurry. He smiled a poker player's smile and Ellie knew she'd get only what he wanted to give.

'So no one thought my father could have — '

'The watu killed her. God knows she had it coming. You can't treat people that badly and get away with it.'

Ruth interceded at last. 'Your father, yes, he drank, and no one blames your mother for leaving. But it's just not right to go around implying that he was somehow involved in that woman's death. That's just not what happened.'

What Ellie felt was a closing-in sensation, the air compressing around her. The certainty of what her father had done despite what they said. And *because* of it. Because they needed it to be a certain way. She put her drink down. 'I should go.'

'No, no, please stay for lunch.' Ruth was trying to be kind, but that was all, a practice of manners. 'We've a lovely roast.'

Ellie stood. Berry looked up at her with his careful eyes. 'You can't know what it was like. You were a child, you still are.'

'Darling, please,' Ruth soothed.

'No,' said Berry. 'She comes here with this idea in her head, basically accusing her own father of murder. And us of collusion. I know the look, every liberal, hairy-legged Peace Corps do-gooder has the same look. We are rich and white in Africa so we must be bad. Well, you should think about how hard we worked. We made farms from raw bush, we built railroads and airports, we founded newspapers and businesses — your father, myself, our fathers before us. And we did it without bank loans or insurance or government hand-outs. No one bailed us out if the rains failed or the locusts came. We were pioneers and we worked our guts out. What you see now,' he waved at the lawn, the quiet afternoon, 'is bought and paid for.'

He wasn't about to give up, just taking another sip. 'We established the game parks. All the animals are here because of us. The Africans would have finished them off by now, every last one, you can be sure of that. It's all nyama to them. We don't hate this government because it's black. We hate it because it has failed, failed all of us, white, black, brown, failed to uphold even the most basic civil rights and to maintain the most basic infrastructure. These bloody idiots took this fantastic country that had everything

— beauty, a great people, natural resources, tourism, tea, coffee, you name it — and turned it into an impoverished shit-hole.'

He leaned back, jiggled his glass, and Daniel dutifully appeared.

23

Your father is throwing stones at the car. He is also screaming. 'You bitch, you fucking bitch,' which are very bad words. You are driving away with Mum in her blue car and then he comes running out of the house. At first you wave but then he bends down and picks up gravel from the driveway and throws it at the car and it thunks against the back window. 'You fucking bitch!'

Mum keeps driving. Pious has the gate open, she drives out and right, past the mango lady and the man who sells cigarettes and bubble gum. Something is wrong with her, she is shaking. Just past the coffee farm she stops the car. Her head falls forward onto the steering wheel. She isn't crying, just moaning like her stomach hurts.

'Mum?'

She says, 'Put your seatbelt on.'

'Mum, where are we going?'

Maybe to the hospital. Maybe she is sick.

'I don't know.' She looks up, leaning her chin on her hands on top of the steering wheel.

First, she drives to Sylvia Leclair's house.

Sylvia isn't expecting Mum but she says, come in, have a cup. You go in with Mum. Sylvia's furniture is covered in plastic. You eat a dry biscuit and stare through the plastic at the peach-coloured velvet beneath. You want to touch the velvet, feel its softness against your legs instead of the plastic that squeaks, or, if you aren't careful, sounds like little farts.

Sylvia is saying, 'Oh, Helen, I wish I could help.'

Mum is saying, 'Just for tonight.'

'I just can't, I'm so sorry, but I know what Wheezie will say. It will make things difficult.'

Sylvia says it's okay for Mum to use the phone, so she goes to use the phone while you stay in the living room with Sylvia. Beside you on the table is a china lady in a yellow dress with a bonnet. You reach out to touch it.

'Don't touch it!' says Sylvia.

So you don't.

She smiles.

Next, you and Mum drive all the way to Mbagathi Ridge, to some old people you don't know. They are friends of Great Aunt B, who you only sort of remember and who sends postcards from Rhodesia. They have a spare bedroom with pink counterpanes on the beds and the bath is also pink with a fluffy cover on the loo seat. Mum says the two of you are going to stay with them for a few days, with Mr and Mrs Alton.

'Why?'

'Because we can't live with your father anymore.'

You look at your mother and she is afraid. Afraid of your father. Does she know? Is this why she ran away? Because he was coming for her?

His footsteps in the dark.

Your mother's eyes will be bulging out.

Then he will come for you.

'When can I see Rosa?' You want to know. She will protect you.

Mum says, 'When we're settled.'

You stay with the Altons for a week. You have no clothes but Mrs Alton has some old clothes that belong to her grandson. You don't like wearing someone else's clothes, especially some boy with short legs, but what else can you do? Mrs Alton is very nice, she bakes a chocolate cake just for you. But Mr Alton is strange, he never remembers who you are or why you are in his house. He's old, he forgets, says Mrs Alton. But every few hours?

Mum finds a maisonette to live in near town with two bedrooms. One day she comes with some things from home, some clothes and dolls, books and pictures. She seems very happy, like it's Christmas and you should be excited. But these are your own things, school uniforms and shoes and sweaters, not presents. You want the treasure box, but it's buried by the sacred tree, only you know where. You ask about Rosa. Mum says, 'Rosa is still working for your father. I can't afford to pay her.'

After a while you move again to a flat in a building where mostly Africans live. They stare at you and run away if you come close. The hallways smell of burnt mealie and posho and LUX soap. Mum says, 'It's okay to live like this.' She even cooks beans and rice like the Africans. You sleep in the same room with her and often there is no hot water. Sometimes no water at all. She has a job at a kindergarten in Westlands, and if you are sick or there is no school you go with her and have to sit quietly with a book in the corner.

A whole year later there is half of a house in Kabete on a steep hill. Rivers of mud wash away the garden Mum plants. You find the flowers in the muddy stream all the way at the bottom of the hill. Gus comes one day to take Mum to a lunch party. She looks beautiful in a yellow dress with pink lipstick and pearl earrings. Gus shakes your hand and says, Hi, how do you do. He is tall with masses of grey hair and a big nose. He is American and you've never met one before.

After that he comes around a lot and Mum is happier, not crying all the time, getting angry and then crying.

Gus brings you a T-shirt that says 'New York Yankees'. He teaches you the American national anthem. He says, 'Neat' a lot. For instance, he says, 'Hey, that's neat.' Which it isn't because it's a collage. But you like him. He talks to you.

You and Mum go to his house for brunch. He explains that brunch is breakfast and lunch altogether, like a lion and a zebra might be a libra or a zebon. You have a laugh and make up names together. Crocant. Elephile.

He has a huge house, bigger even than your home, which isn't your home any more. His cook makes sandwiches layered with ham and cheese so that you can hardly open your mouth wide enough to take a bite. Gus says that Americans invented sandwiches.

Then he says, 'How would you like to live in America?'

You want to ask, 'Can Rosa come?' But you already know she won't.

So you ask for the next best thing: 'Can I have a horse?'

'Yes,' says Gus.

'A real one, not a toy one?'

Gus and Mum laugh. You are glad you've made them laugh even if you don't know why. You don't know the why of any of it. Why has the world rotated and gravity lost its pull so things and people fall off and disappear?

24

The phone rang in her room. 'There is a lady here to see you.'

'Who?'

The receptionist struggled with a name. Ellie spared her. 'I'll be right down.'

As she stepped out of the elevator, an elderly woman came forward. She wore a floral-print dress and a cardigan. Her hair was steel-grey. She was too thin. 'I probably should have called but I live not very far from here, it's on my way,' she said. 'I have to go to Hurlingham for a hair appointment.'

Her speech was hesitant, almost a stutter, and Ellie saw she kept her left hand in her dress pocket to hide the tremor.

'I'm Eleanor.'

'I know. I'm Jean, Jean Gallagher. I'd like to talk, if you have a minute. I just happened to phone Ruth Harrison last night, we belong to the same book club you see, and she mentioned that you were here.' She smiled briefly, so Ellie would know this was a friendly visit. 'I was John's first wife, your father's first wife.'

They sat in the dining room as the last of

breakfast was cleared away, the four crois-
sants and three Danishes that had survived
the church convention, the three German
tour groups and several airline crews.

'You look like him,' Jean said. 'Everyone
says that, don't they?'

'Only here. Everywhere else I look like my
mother.'

'That's not quite right, is it? Of course, I
know what you mean. I often wonder, if we'd
had a child, what she or he would have
looked like. That's part of the reason I came,
I must confess. I wanted to see his child. To
see him again.'

'I'm not him.'

Jean dipped her eyes to her coffee. 'You're
quite wrong, you know. About your father.
What Ruth was saying, that you think he had
something to do with Maria Riktoffen's
death.' She looked up. 'Do you think that?'

Ellie noticed a smudge of food encrusted
on Jean's cardigan. Her clothes were worn.
There was no housegirl to clean them any
more, there was no money and no privilege
left in her life. Ellie felt sorry for her. 'I have
some questions about it, yes.'

'He wasn't like that. I mean he was odd, he
was remote. I couldn't reach him and I don't
think your mother could. He was separate
— how can I explain it — he wasn't quite

here with the rest of us. He was . . . he was in exile. The landscape around him was always foreign. But that's not quite right. Because he was born here, well, in Dar, and he was very good with the Africans, they liked him, the ones he worked with, in business. He didn't see colour, it didn't matter to him. But then, what did? Apart from the drink.'

'When you say, 'He wasn't like that,' I'm not sure what you mean,' Ellie said.

'He wasn't violent.'

'You weren't his child.'

Jean put her cup down and tried to still her trembling hand. 'I'm sorry,' she said. 'He hit you?'

Ellie turned away.

Was that the word for it? Hitting? When did hitting become beating? She felt Jean's cool hand on top of hers, just a light touch, a pat, and something contracted in her throat, or lodged there. She swallowed hard.

'It wasn't just Maria Riktoffen,' she said. 'There was Eileen McMullen.'

'Eileen? The doctor's wife?'

'She didn't kill herself.'

Jean was silent a moment. 'Why are you doing this?'

'You came here to tell me how wonderful he was.'

'No, not wonderful,' Jean said. 'But not like

you're making him, some kind of . . . I don't know, monster.'

She went on: 'When I heard he was getting remarried, I thought, poor woman. But then I thought, maybe it'll work. Your mother was so young and pretty. I think he really wanted to do right by her. Between us there had been too much drink, you see, too many parties. But with Helen, I thought, maybe he'll straighten up. He was so handsome, so brilliantly intelligent, and what a waste.' She looked out at the swimming pool as if searching for someone.

'Whatever he did to you was terrible — I can't imagine — but it wasn't out of the ordinary. So many children here were shunted off to ayahs or boarding schools, out of the way, so the adults could carry on. That was his own childhood, too. Spanking a child, hitting a child, everyone did it.'

Ellie's voice rose against her will: 'You absolve him so easily.'

'It was different then.'

'That is what Berry said.'

Jean's gaze was very still. 'I can't bear to think of him raising his hand to a child, to you, to any child. I can't bear to think of the pain he caused you. But also the pain he was in. What he did to you, it wasn't anything to do with you, anything you did. It wasn't because of you. Can you understand that? It doesn't change what he did or make it less. I'm not saying that. But his violence was inward and whoever he took into his heart was subject to his despair.'

Ellie lowered her eyes. She saw Eileen McMullen's body, the sash around her neck, and thought, she too was subject to his despair. All of us. Subjects of his despair. Even you, Jean, with your lingering love.

'I must go,' Jean said. 'I'm already late.'

They stood. Ellie walked with her to the hotel entrance. Neither said a word. Then Jean squeezed her arm. Her hand was thin and cold. 'You're like him. You take it inside you. Don't.'

An ancient Renault 4 pulled up, an old African at the wheel. He got out, opened the passenger door for Jean. She smiled at Ellie, then got in. 'Thank you, Christopher,' she said to the old man. The two of them drove away, the small white car merging into the frantic highway traffic.

25

Helen heard the door slam and then John yelling: 'Rosa!' Running downstairs, she found John in the hallway outside his study. She'd never seen him so angry. 'Someone's been messing around in my desk,' he said.

'But no one has a key to your study,' Helen said.

John looked at her. 'Did you hear what I said?'

Rosa appeared, standing nervously in the doorway that went through to the kitchen. Her hands twisted the edges of her apron. John turned to her, 'Have you been in my study?'

She shook her head. 'Hapana.'

'The things in my desk, my papers and letters have been moved around,' he said.

'Hapana.'

'Who else has a key? You? Sam? The memsahib?'

Helen said, 'No one has a key, only you. Rosa only cleans in there when you open it for her.'

'So the things in my desk just moved around by themselves?'

Helen thought: you moved them yourself when you were drunk and now you don't remember. Like when the car was 'stolen' and then you found it at the Club. Or the money missing from your wallet because you couldn't remember picking up the bar tab at the Norfolk.

He pushed past her and yelled up the stairs: 'Eleanor!'

Helen grabbed his arm, 'She can't get in, it's not her!'

He said, 'She's always playing sneaky buggers.'

Ellie was at the top of the stairs. She's so thin, Helen thought, where does it go, all that food? She eats and eats and still she looks like an African child, barefoot and bony-kneed. Her hair, unbrushed, was spun gold, arcing out from her head like a sparkler on Guy Fawkes.

'It's not her!' Helen said, tightening her grip.

'Don't,' he said.

She stepped back.

John looked up at Ellie: 'Come here.'

Helen grabbed him again, 'It's nothing to do with her. I did it, it was me.'

He hadn't drunk enough. This was why Helen never had Ellie's friends to play. If he hadn't drunk enough, or if he had drunk too much he would shout at them. Be quiet! Go to your room!

'Get your hands off me,' he said to her. And she did, because she couldn't stop him with her hands or her words. Instead she watched Ellie come slowly down the stairs. He'll just shout at her, she told herself. He'll accuse her and shout at her and send her to her room.

Ellie reached the bottom step and crossed the red Persian carpet. Without warning John took his daughter in one hand, and spun her so she half lay on the hall table, then he beat her small bottom with his hand. It all happened so fast, like watching a car crash, when the horror of the act stuns the viewer so he cannot move. The brain takes moments to understand what is actually happening. Years later, Helen read about an attack on a bus; a gang of youths attacked the conductor and ripped his eyes out while the other passengers stood by; one witness was quoted as saying: 'It just didn't seem real.' Atrocities are committed in the moment between the real and the unreal, between dream and waking, when the scream dries on your tongue.

The telephone fell on the floor with a smash and a little ring. John released Ellie. She stood and half turned, her dress still half hitched behind her, her eyes looking away, out the door to the bright day. John staggered a step. 'Go to your room,' he said.

Whenever Helen recalled the attack, the worst part was the beginning, when he made Eleanor walk down the stairs and across the red carpet toward him, making her walk toward her future, for he knew what he was going to do and so did she. They both understood the submission the walk required, the humiliation it guaranteed.

Ellie did as he said and went quietly up the stairs. Helen started up after her, but John said: 'Leave her.' For a moment she obeyed, but she was ashamed of herself for behaving like an accomplice. Then she pushed past him and ran up the stairs. Ellie was in her room, lying on her bed, on her side. Helen sat beside her and stroked her hair. She said nothing — what could words do now?

After a while she lay down next to her daughter, spooning her body into hers. But immediately she felt she was trespassing, she was not welcome. Helen understood that Ellie was sealed up. Silence was her revenge. There would be no tears, no hugs. And why, Helen thought, why should my child seek comfort in my arms? I have betrayed her. Why can I neither prevent her pain, nor cure it?

Helen lay there, helpless, listening to her

daughter breathe. Sound was layered in the still room, Ellie's breathing, and outside, birdsong, traffic, a radio playing in the servants' quarters. When she was sure Ellie was asleep, she rose and left the room, carefully closing the door behind her. Downstairs, she found Rosa in the kitchen washing dishes.

'She's okay,' Helen said.

Rosa kept her eyes on the dishes.

'She'll be okay, she'll forget all about it,' Helen said.

Rosa put away the cutlery and the plates.

That afternoon, John drove off, tearing out of the driveway in a back-spray of gravel. Several hours later he came back. Helen was in the spare room sewing name tags on Ellie's school uniform, the blue socks and dark red jerseys. She heard him come up the stairs, and knew by his fumbling tread that he'd stopped by the Club.

She saw him go to Ellie's room and knock on the door.

'Eleanor?' he said.

He had bought her presents, an assortment of cheap Maasai beaded bracelets, a dozen of the little wooden animal carvings that were sold in curio shops, a book about airplanes, a doll in plastic wrapping, and a chocolate bar.

Ellie was sitting on the floor, looking up at him.

'I thought you might like these,' he said.

She stood and took them one by one. 'Thank you.'

'What are you drawing?' he said.

'Horses.'

He looked down. 'That's very good.'

'Thank you.'

'Well,' he said.

Don't turn away, don't walk out, Helen willed. Please. Put out your hand, touch her hair or face.

But he walked out. And Helen felt not that things were falling apart, but that they were folding in on each other, the tighter and tighter folds of some absurdly complex origami. Each fold was the end of an opportunity for the design to become something beautiful: a bird, a cat, a flower, a loving family. Was that life? The ceaseless narrowing of opportunities, the fold upon fold, exposed surfaces constrained into complexity, until, suffocating, there was no surface left to catch the light.

26

What is a bloodbath?

You think of red blood like paint in a white bath.

In Uganda, there is a bloodbath.

Idi Amin is making people kill each other under the mango trees. It is a game. You have to kill the other person, you have to smash in his skull or he will smash in yours. There are bodies rotting in the bean fields, some are children's bodies. Lake Victoria is full of bodies. The crocodiles are happy. There is a hotel in Kampala where people are made to jump from the top floor. There is another hotel that leaks blood and screams.

You are sitting with Baptist listening to Voice of Kenya. The Asians have been expelled from Uganda, as if from school, and you wonder, what have they done wrong? Most of the white farmers have also left, fearing for their lives. The borders at Malaba and Busiu are crowded with people trying to leave Uganda and come to Kenya.

'Why is Idi Amin killing all these people?' you ask Baptist. 'Are they bad people?'

'Because he is a madman,' says Baptist.

'They are innocent people, they have done nothing. He is crazy. You must stop him. Your government must send in their army.'

You think a bloodbath is when they kill people with pangas in a large bathroom and drain their blood into the bath. Idi Amin takes a bath in the blood. But the British army will stop him, they will arrest him and put him in jail. A British solider will take the plug out of the bath, the blood will drain away. The bodies will be buried, the graves will be covered with flowers.

VoK ends the news: 'Keep on keeping on.' Maendeleo.

In the middle of the night, Great Aunt B and Great Uncle Stanley arrive in their Land Rover, full up with suitcases and boxes and dogs. You are supposed to be asleep, but you listen on the stairs.

'Only what we have in the car,' says Great Aunt B. 'The servants were lined up with their children and suitcases. They expected us to take them with us! It was dreadful, we had to leave everything, my mother's piano, Stanley's desk lamp, family heirlooms.'

Great Uncle Stanley says nothing, you can almost see his silence as well as hear it. You peek. He is drinking, staring at the patterns on the carpet.

'We have no money,' says Great Aunt B.

'Just what we had in the safe, a few hundred pounds. Everything else is in the bank in Kampala and you can bet that's as good as gone.

'We saw bodies on the side of the road. School children, pregnant women, anyone. A pile of bodies, children from the secondary school in Jinja. I recognized the uniforms. At the road blocks the soldiers were shooting people, just when they felt like it, for fun.

'They took everything from the Asians, sometimes even their cars, and made them walk. They didn't kill them, though, just the Africans, just each other. We thought after the Asians they'd leave us alone. They have the nerve to call it 'Nationalization', but it's just theft, plain and simple.

'The estate is still ours, legally, if that means anything to those monkeys. Not like the Asians who had to sign over their property deeds. When this all calms down Stanley says we can go back. But I don't want to. I keep saying we should go to Rhodesia. Ian Smith knows which way is up. Good old Smithie will keep the country white. Stanley has so much experience, he'll get a job managing a farm in no time, and we can work our way up again to our own farm. Maybe tobacco. Or maybe we'll buy a small hotel up-country. I'd like that. Stanley's keen to look here, but I'm against it. You just can't trust these bloody munts. It'll happen here, mark my words.'

You dream that it happens here. Idi Amin comes for you, up the stairs, you can hear him with his panga. He has red eyes and is laughing. He takes you into the bathroom and you see the bath is already full of blood. You wonder whose blood. And you see Rosa's Salvation Army hat on the floor. Just the Africans, they kill just the Africans. And you are an African. Your skin is black — how did that happen? — and you are trying to tell Idi Amin that you are white, really you are mzungu, therefore you cannot be killed.

27

She opened a bottle of whisky from the mini-bar. She had never liked whisky and never liked being drunk, the lack of control. She wondered why it appealed to him, the disorder of drink, the sloppiness. She poured the Scotch the way he did, on the rocks with a dash of water. It was bitter but she persevered.

On the table by the window lay the photograph her mother gave her: the boy on the dock, Dar es Salaam, 1928. As her mother would have it, where it all began. Or as Jean would perhaps have suggested, the beginning of his exile.

She took another sip. Johnny Walker Red. Not his brand. She couldn't remember which was. But she remembered the ritual, the clink of ice cubes, the water, the swirling in the glass. How much had he drunk? A bottle a day at least. A litre a day. 365 litres a year. For twenty, thirty, forty years. Enough to fill a swimming pool.

When he drank at home he simply drank, steadfastly attacking the task of obliteration in his armchair. But when he drank at the Club, did he talk with other drinkers, with, say, Berry? Did he laugh, tell jokes? Did he reach a calm, smooth place deep in the amber womb of the bottle?

Did he forget?

Did his crimes evaporate with the ice?

Once he had been a boy, blameless and afraid. Once he had been a man, tall and finely cut. He had desired something other than whisky and silence: a woman's skin, the groove of her back. Once, there had been no excuses to make. He and Helen, he and Jean, Berry and Ruth, Maria and Nels, they had walked like kings and queens across the land. They had been pure of heart. But mistakes were made, accidents, bad choices. Too much drink. The excuses became a way of preserving their purity of intention, their innocence. And eventually of perpetuating the rightness of their regime.

It was different then.

How different for Baptist? Was his pain different because he was black? Did his children die differently to white children? How different for Rosa? How was her poverty different? Different for every shamba boy or houseboy who went to prison for stealing sugar? Did their bones break differently?

It was different then. Mrs McMullen killed

herself because she was crazy. Maria Riktoffen had it coming to her. And the poet of
numbers had a gift they all needed: he could
make money disappear here and reappear
there. It was different then, when children
should be seen and not heard.

28

Sunday is Rosa's day off. As a member of the Salvation Army, she dedicates this day to them. Mum has given her a new Salvation Army uniform for Christmas. It hangs in a special place in Rosa's room, covered in dry-cleaner's plastic, waiting. Early Sunday morning Rosa heats water in her kettle and fills a bucket and washes. You know this because if you go round to the servants' quarters at seven, Rosa will be wearing Mum's old blue dressing gown, and she will smell of Imperial Leather soap. The bucket of suds and murky water will still be steaming.

The servants' quarters is a block of three rooms with no windows, just doors. There is a strip of cement in front of the rooms, then tightly packed dirt that Rosa or Sam sweeps every morning and every evening. Beyond lies a field of maize and beans which they plant and harvest. There is an outdoor tap and sink at one end of the block, and some distance off is the choo. The choo always smells. Other smells you notice are burnt mealie, Rosa's 'White Night' perfume, the chickens, and mostly the dark, bitter smell of Pious. The place smells of Pious even when he isn't there, and you can locate him anywhere in the garden from downwind.

Once you asked Mum why Pious smells. She said some Africans didn't understand about washing, they didn't have access to water. You said, but I know he washes. Mum said, Well, then, I don't know, it's just the way it is, but don't ask him, he'll be very insulted.

You asked Rosa instead. And she wouldn't tell you either.

Rosa makes you tea, milky and thick with sugar. The sugar is coarse and doesn't dissolve completely, so the tea becomes sweeter and sweeter the more you drink until the last few gulps are a kind of gritty syrup. As you drink your tea, Rosa prepares for the Salvation Army. She keeps her best shoes under the bed in a shoe box. You help Rosa shine the shoes to a pitch gloss. The soles are worn in places, so Rosa has stuffed newspaper inside, and the leather around the toes has been repaired with big, clumsy stitches.

You ask Rosa why she doesn't buy new shoes. Rosa shakes her head and makes her 'Ai, ai, ai' sound which means you don't understand anything.

On Sundays Rosa stands in front of the mirror and plucks out her silver hairs. The hairs are coiled and springy and look like mini-Slinkys. She then rubs Vaseline on her legs and arms. She shines.

When the final moment arrives, Rosa makes you turn away. You stare at a framed picture of Jesus with a multicoloured halo and sad blue eyes. It is the only picture Rosa has. You wonder why she doesn't have pictures of her children in Kisumu. She has six. You have only met one, the oldest, Augustine, who came here once. Mum gave him a school satchel exactly like yours. Augustine said 'Thank you' in the softest voice. You wanted to show him the garden but Rosa said no, he must stay with her in the servants' quarters and do his schoolwork. Mum told you that Rosa paid for Augustine to go to a good school, she wanted her son to be educated and get a good job, maybe in a bank or as a teacher.

There is a rustle of plastic. Then she says, 'Aya, teyari.' You turn back around and fasten the row of buttons up the back of Rosa's dress for her, just the way Rosa fastens the buttons on your school uniform every morning. Underneath Rosa wears a white slip with lace edging. You finish the buttons and Rosa stands straight in the mirror. She brushes the fabric smooth; it is so white against her black skin, and her teeth when she parts her lips to smile at her reflection are like pearls. Last of all is the hat, a white headscarf with a high, starched maroon-coloured crown. Gold letters stencilled across the maroon say: SALVATION ARMY. Maroon is also the colour of your school sweater and blazer.

The Salvation Army gatherings take place all over Nairobi. Sometimes it takes Rosa hours to get there. On those days she leaves before the sun comes up. How does she keep her outfit clean on those dirty buses?

But today, Rosa has told you they are going to march on the road right by the house.

You wait. You sit on a stone at the bottom of the driveway for hours, long hours: the smaller you are the bigger time is. Cars pass, a dog barks, the sun flickers through the wavy fronds of the pepper tree. You wonder what would happen if you look directly at the sun. Alison Chester said your eyeballs will start bleeding and you will go blind. You try to look at the sun but can't. Bleeding eyeballs probably hurt quite a lot.

Then you hear them: a drumbeat a long way off, beyond the police station. As they come closer you can hear singing. Over the crest of the hill they march, fifty of them, with big drums, cans filled with stones that make a scratchy sound, and a trumpet. The man at the front has the trumpet and he marches with straight legs, kicking one out in front of the other. Some of them don't have uniforms, just their church clothes. They sing in Swahili, songs about God, nothing like the hymns you sing at school assembly, but then at school there aren't any drums or a trumpet or cans of stones, there is only mean Mr Williams plinkety-plinking on the piano and 'All Things Bright And Beautiful'. These songs are marching songs, 'Onward Christian Soldiers', praying to God songs, and they sing them for hours and over miles of hot, sticky tarmac.

You search the white uniforms for Rosa. She is in the middle, holding a pair of big brass cymbals. Baptist is beside her, singing. She must be important, you think, because no one else has cymbals, most people have cans of stones, Baptist is just singing. You see Rosa smash the cymbals together and hope — hope and pray — everyone knows that Rosa is your friend.

But Rosa doesn't see you, she marches and sings, she is almost past you, past the house, and you will her to turn and look. And Rosa does. She smiles, Baptist smiles and waves. You wave back.

You keep waving as Rosa and Baptist march on down the dip and up the other side, miles from anywhere, from the main road, from anyone else who might watch or listen, unless there are other children like you standing at the edge of the road waiting for their friends to pass.

29

She was surrounded by the dead and the failing. O'Shea, Berry Harrison, Richard Boudreau, Jean Gallagher. They were no longer the beautiful swingers, the barbarous acolytes of colonial power. Time had disrobed them of glamour and force, made them hard to hate. But Ellie thought of Berry's enduring arrogance and what he had willed himself to remember and what to forget. How he rearranged the past, like furniture, to suit his needs, to preserve his view of the hills. She thought of O'Shea taking prisoners into the woods.

There was one last name, one last person to whom Ellie hoped she could turn. In her memory he appeared a gentler spirit — though distracted, peripheral. With sweets in his pocket. With his crest of grey hair, running into the house, to his dead wife.

The phone book yielded not a single McMullen, so she went to Nairobi Hospital, a private hospital, not the rat- and faeces-infested government hospital of Julius Mwangi's shame. This, however, was just across the street. And outside the bleak, weather-stained building, women in second-hand clothing and fraying kitenges, men in Oxfam trousers waited amid a ghostly swirl of dust and blue plastic bags. They would have no experience of the clean, white hallways of Nairobi Hospital down which Ellie was led by a young administrative assistant in a pink uniform and matching pink nail polish. They would have no notion of the existence of the gift shop, the orderly pushing a book-loan cart, the tender mercy of expensive painkillers and antibiotics.

'Oh, he was one of our doctors. I remember him,' Ester from Human Resources told Ellie. 'He was a very nice man, a dear man, a good doctor. But it has been some time. Fifteen, maybe twenty years. I had just started my job.'

Ellie asked for his address, if it was possible.

Ester filtered through several filing cabinets. 'I'm not supposed to. But he's no longer practising here. I'm looking through our pension payments. If we have anything, if he has not passed on, he will be receiving his pension. It will be noted here.'

30

The first time John decided to stop drinking he and Helen went to Naivasha, just the two of them. They rented the Caldicotts' farm on the northern end of the lake. Helen told Roy of the plan, and Roy said 'Good for him,' though with a surprising lack of enthusiasm. He warned Helen that the first few days would be difficult. He prescribed some tranquillizers and said they would keep John calm, they would help him sleep. He put his hand on her shoulder, 'It's difficult what he's trying to do. What you are trying to help him do. Don't be disappointed if it doesn't work.'

That made her angry, that pessimism, that lack of faith.

Before they left the house John had one for the road, so that he could actually hold the steering wheel.

The road cut along the side of the Escarpment. They were almost airborne on the thin strip of tarmac and Helen tried to quell her fear. To the left the cliff dropped away hundreds of feet. To the right were signs warning of falling rocks. And coming towards them were insane bus drivers, lorries overtaking on blind curves.

But John was talking, chatting, something he never did. He was telling her about office politics, some gossip from the Club. She knew he was nervous, and that must be a good thing. He was taking this dry-out seriously. He even squeezed her hand. 'It'll be all right,' he said. She remembered those other words of his from long ago now, that other promise: 'It'll get better.'

Down along the south side of the lake, they turned onto a rough dirt road. The lakeside was green, lush with long grass and yellow fever trees. A half-mile back from the water, the green yielded abruptly to desert, to cactus, rock, and whistling thorn. Helen thought with excitement of the birdlife she'd find here, water birds, woodland birds and desert birds. She had her binoculars with her and her bird book. This week she would go for walks, she might even find species she hadn't seen before, a collared sunbird, a lammergeyer.

'We could move here. What do you think?' John said. 'I could farm — dairy cows, maybe beans. That would be good, wouldn't it?'

Helen didn't resist the images that were suddenly there in her head, unbidden but clear, as if they'd been waiting for the light, for an open window: how it would be, how happy Ellie would be here, they all would be. John would be outside, busy with the farm, active all day and too tired for drink, too healthy for it. And Ellie would have a pony, she'd ride all over the farm, galloping bareback along the lake shore. Helen would become the cook she'd always wanted to be, and she'd take up sewing and learn Swahili properly, maybe even open a school for the farm children.

'It would. It would be wonderful,' she said.

He took his eyes off the road for a moment to look at her, to see her there beside him with her brown hair and her dark eyes. How badly he wanted to deserve her.

'Of course I'd have to hire a good manager who could teach me. Maybe Stanley, if they're not too settled in Salisbury. And we'd have to cut down on our expenses.'

'I don't expect we'd have as many,' Helen said. 'We'd get our food from the farm or locally. I could make my clothes, and Ellie's.'

'I could always work part time, a few days in Nairobi, then the rest of the time up here. Just to keep my hand in. I am a partner, after all, I can't just run off and live in the bush.' He rested his elbow out the window as if the dust and the sun were his elements.

★ ★ ★

They arrived at about one, filthy from the dust but still exhilarated by the landscape and their plans. The house perched atop a hill, overlooking the smaller of Naivasha's two lakes and crowded round with fever trees. The trees were full of yellow weaverbirds who were forever building delicate basket-like nests. Their chatter overlaid the sharp spur of cicadas and the sound of farm machinery, a tractor perhaps, working the fields behind the house.

The rooms were bright and open, full of comfy sofas and big pillows. Looking around, Helen knew that this was the life she was supposed to have. For so long it was as if there had been a mistake, similar suitcases switched at the airport perhaps, but finally the right one had been returned to her.

Helen found the cook and told him the supplies were in the car and that he could make sandwiches for lunch. She and the bwana would be on the veranda. As she turned away from him, she said: 'Is there anything to drink in the house? Any alcohol — whisky, gin?'

The cook told her it was in the drinks cabinet in the dining room. And this was where she found John. Surveying the rows of bottles, he said, 'I think we'd better get rid of all this.' He and Helen carried the bottles ceremoniously into the kitchen and put them on the table.

John told the cook: 'Take the bottles, store them and guard them. We don't want them in the house while we are here. But at the end of the week, they must be full, like now. Sawa?'

The cook nodded solemnly, 'Sawa, Bwana,' and put the bottles in a box.

Half an hour later, he brought lunch onto the veranda: chicken salad sandwiches, potato crisps and passionfruit juice. John would have loved a beer, he was aching for one, cold and amber with a good head on it, heaven in a glass. Helen could tell what he was thinking, she saw how he jiggled his leg and tapped his fingers on the table.

'How about one of those pills?' he said when they'd finished the food.

Helen found them in her handbag. 'Why don't you go and have a nice kip?' she said. 'You deserve it after that long drive.' Keep him doped up, Roy had said. Try and get him to sleep through the first seventy-two hours, they'll be the worst.

⋆ ⋆ ⋆

He said: 'The single malt.'

It was the middle of the night and he wasn't sleeping so neither was she.

'Just a glass, that's all I need.'

'The cook has it,' she said. 'I can't go and get it now.'

He was pacing.

'Send the askari. He can wake the bastard up. He's probably drinking it himself.'

Helen lay there and closed her eyes.

John kicked the bed.

'Wake up!'

She opened her eyes.

'Stupid bitch.'

He was sweating, standing, an arm flailing.

'Get me a fucking drink.'

He was half-shadow, half-man, moving between the moon-filled windows of the dark room.

'Get me a fucking drink!'

He would not hurt her, somehow she knew that, somehow she was inviolable.

'Stop,' he said and pressed the heels of his hands against his temples. 'Stop.'

She got out of bed. 'What is it?'

He looked at her without recognition and she thought he must be in some other place, the country of his past, a nationstate that existed and was not memory but terrain, cities, tombs.

She took his hand, bringing him back from the dead. 'John, it's okay, I'm here.'

He lay down. She put cold flannels on his

forehead. She covered him with blankets. And later she helped him to the toilet.

'I don't know whether to shit or puke,' he said.

She held a bowl to his mouth so he could do both.

He leaned against her as they walked back to bed. If I had to, she thought, I could carry him. I'm strong enough.

'Hold me,' he said. And she did.

★   ★   ★

He had nightmares whenever he fell asleep, not just once in a while. He woke up crying, screaming, groping for her, a rock in the terrible current of his dreams. She held him, soothed him.

'Perhaps if we talk about it the dreams will stop,' she said. 'They say that about dreams, don't they, if you tell them to someone you don't have them again.'

He pushed her away, rolled onto his side, his back to her.

'I don't dream,' he said. 'I remember.'

Why would he not share this with her — isn't that what husbands and wives did with their troubles? Was it the war? She had only threads, carefully gleaned: the falling plane, how the dead bloated in the tropical heat, even though alive they had been so thin. Maybe that was why he wouldn't speak of it to her — what could she know or understand of horror and fear? Her ignorance reminded him of all that he could never un-know.

He had medals, but he never wore them. He was not like other war heroes she knew who kept up with their squadrons and went to reunions. He never told stories of derring-do or of close escapes. During the day, he went to work, he tallied figures, he devised systems, he had lunch, played golf. But at night he fell seaward in a burning plane.

★   ★   ★

By the third day he was sleeping better, the nightmares abated and he could keep food down. After lunch, Helen left him in the cool, whitewashed bedroom with the blue cotton curtains drawn against the afternoon light. She walked away from the house, down the hill, toward the lake. It was hot, sweat pricked under her arms and along her forehead under her hat, and soundless, but for the cicadas. The blue lake shimmered beyond the tall reeds. All other colour had withdrawn from the landscape, retreated into the green shade of the acacias.

Helen followed a cow path that vaguely rimmed the lake. She planned to walk north and then cut back toward the farm after an hour and be back in time for tea. This was not the best time for birding but she felt she had more leeway for exploration. In the evening she wouldn't dare to strike out into the bush like this as hippos came ashore to graze and leopards slipped down from their trees to hunt. Now she just had to keep a wary eye out for buffalo and chose paths through open ground. Whenever she did walk through an area of scrub, she felt her body tense and her senses sharpen as eyes, ears, nose and brain scanned the air for the presence of some hulking, grey beast. Passing into the open again, she felt a small thrill of victory, as if she'd cheated one of those old brutes by slipping past unnoticed.

She veered back from the lake and found herself in a narrow gully with high, stony sides. There was no danger of buffalo here — they didn't like the rough, closed ground. It wasn't beautiful, not for someone with English eyes, but she was filled with wonder at the structure of the land, as if the rocks were the bones of the earth and the roots of trees its ligaments. In the rainy season water coursed through here and smoothed the stones and pooled in hollows. Now, the stones were steps for her or perches for lizards. In the cool rock underpinnings she knew there must be snakes, and in the scrubby bundu birds waited for their evensong.

Around her was a private world that didn't care who she was or what mistakes she made, but accepted her. This was the Africa she wanted, not the claustrophobia of Nairobi, the bitchy gossip behind high walls, her own unhappy marriage. Perhaps it might be her Africa after all.

She walked on, knowing she should turn back, she was already late. After another twenty minutes, the gully began to shallow out and she rose up again into the landscape. She was surrounded by candelabra trees and in the distance she could see a herd of zebra moving across open ground in the direction of the lake.

The sky was cooling, the shadows gaining ground. She sat on the bare earth, with her back against a tree. She wanted to always be this still, wanted the sun to wait and the world to hold its pose. And just then, as she exhaled, a single male impala stepped into the space between the trees. He had not seen her, nor smelled her in the breathless air. He moved on mute hooves, his tail and ears flicking, his dark liquid eyes glancing back toward the open grassland, not yet suspecting her alien presence. And for that moment, Helen felt she was not there, not bodily in the clumsy human form that trips and stamps and crushes, but that she was spirit, unweighted as the sunlight in the trees. In another instant, the impala saw her, or sensed her, and shied away with a sharp bark, and skittered into the open. He looked back at her, as if annoyed that he'd fallen for her ruse of silence, then twitched his tail and watched as she walked away from the copse of trees, following the zebra down toward the lake.

★   ★   ★

When she returned to the house, sunset was only an hour away and she was nervous about John. He'd never have slept so long, even with the pills.

He was awake, drinking tea and reading a book on the veranda.

'Helen.' He rose to greet her. 'Did you have a nice walk?'

For a moment she looked at him, wary of some trick. He reached out and touched her cheek. 'You've caught the sun.'

★   ★   ★

That night they made love. Afterward, he got out of bed and opened the curtains to let in the moonlight.

He said, 'I remember hearing children's voices. They were laughing, playing somewhere beyond the camp. Jock said, 'They're playing Cowboys and Indians.' I said, 'They've never heard of cowboys and the only Indians they know are shopkeepers.' They were island children, they didn't know anything but monsoons and coconuts. They were running and laughing. We listened to them. We listened with our whole bodies, not just our ears, but with our fingertips, the hairs on our arms. We held our breath to listen.'

John raised his fingers to his mouth as if he could feel the words as they came out; and maybe he could catch them and push them back if he needed to.

Helen went to him. She put her arms around him. 'Did that help, hearing them? Did it give you at least a little bit of happiness?'

He said, 'We hadn't heard anything but men's voices for two years. The children — their joy was so disturbing — it terrified us. We were terrified.'

31

The bus took her south through a bone-dry landscape of great beauty and desolation. The Athi Plains flowed outward, a sea of sun-burned grass, past Kitengela, Kajiado, and pale distant hills. But when human habitation intervened on the roadside, Ellie felt herself recoil. Cans, bags, plastic water bottles trooped relentlessly across the dusty earth. Hundreds of people, stoned on hunger, stood or squatted in the wind in front of their shanties. There was nothing for them to do: no work, no rain, no crops, only passing cars, goats, the belligerent wind. Ellie wondered when the hunger became worse than the boredom.

After several hours, there came a clutter of buildings, green fig trees and baobabs, chickens, and camels crossing the road.

'Namanga!' the bus driver announced in his most professional manner — after all this was the 'fancy bus', a late model minibus with upholstery and windows that opened and closed. Only one person per seat and no live animals inside the vehicle. 'Please have your passports and travel documents ready.'

Like all border towns, Namanga was in constant motion: trucks, buses, cars, police, Maasai women hawking beads and carvings, old women selling mealies, Somalis changing money, Indians hiding new electronic equipment under the seats of their Peugeots. Here were scams, smuggled goods, bribes. Here, the impounded vehicle lot probably served as a used parts and secondhand car mart. There were no rules, no laws. The town lay between two countries, was two towns at once, wasn't a town at all but a stop along the way.

Even the people who lived here were drawn into the drama of travelling. Buses and matatus carrying goods and people and stories from afar shaped their way of looking at the world. They knew where to buy cheap stolen mobile phones in Nairobi or Mombasa, or whom to talk to when smuggling goods from Zanzibar to the mainland. They knew without going to such places, for they heard and saw and gleaned a great flotsam of knowledge. They knew the outer world, it was available and familiar to them. Staying was therefore a choice, not a fate.

The bus stopped, the passengers filed out and into the immigration building and passports were exit-stamped. They then drove across the border into Tanzania for entry visas. The driver unloaded the suitcases from the roof. These, he said, would have to be checked by the customs inspector.

Ellie waited with the other passengers in the thin shade of the customs shed. Just beyond the border fence the town ended abruptly and the bush began: miles of acacia scrub and red earth. She sat on her suitcase and fanned herself with a magazine. A barefoot boy came around selling peanuts and bottles of water. A thin cat edged along the shadows and lay on the cool cement.

Thirty, forty, fifty minutes passed in the slow-oozing midday heat. No one complained, for there was no one to complain to, no one who would care. The waiting seemed to be part of the routine. The driver dozed in the bus with a newspaper over his face. It occurred to Ellie that here waiting was an active verb, like running or dancing.

A man on a motorcycle pulled up. The bike was dusty, as was its owner. He took off his helmet. His dark hair was spiky with sweat. He had high cheekbones, a straight nose. Clean lines, blue eyes. He sat down not far from Ellie and took a paperback from his jacket pocket, and read as purposefully as if he was in a library.

A tour bus arrived. The tourists in their immaculate safari outfits disembarked, blinking at the sun and their surroundings. They seemed confused as to why they were here at all, for this was not a hotel or a game park, this hadn't been mentioned in the brochure. Among them Ellie noticed a woman whose attire was absurd — no, more: it was repulsive in its opulence. She was perhaps in her late fifties, well padded and manicured. She wore a spotless white silk jumpsuit and her neck, wrists and waist were coiled with gold.

The woman was careful not to touch anything as she entered the immigration room with her group. Then the group came out and stood with the mounting pile of baggage. Within minutes she began to berate her driver about the wait. The driver, a slender Kenyan in his own careful safari outfit, zebra-print hat at a jaunty angle, explained that there was nothing he could do, the customs inspector would come soon.

But the woman ranted on in her European accent, and when no one offered more than rote sympathy, she broadened the scope of her dissatisfaction: the smell, the crowds, the flies, the shower in the hotel, the food, the heat, the water, the animals.

The driver had heard it all before — there was always one in the group. He nodded, shook his head, made the soft, sympathetic noises he'd learned on his customer care course, but his mind was somewhere in Arusha, later, with his brown girlfriend in a bar, with a cold beer and music from the Congo.

The traffic, the driving, the dust, the woman was saying, this litter, these people.

Ellie studied the hundreds of swifts weaving tapestries in the still air. They nested under a high tin roof that once sheltered a loading bay but was now a kind of picnic area for the truck drivers. They occupied an assortment of faded faux-velvet sofas and broken chairs. The drivers were laughing, the swifts soared and dove, and the words came before Ellie realized, loud enough so everyone could hear.

'You must have been expecting some other Africa,' she said.

The woman turned to her.

'Some other Africa.' Ellie gestured with open hands, her voice pitched with anger. 'Not this one.'

The man with the motorcycle was looking at her. He smiled.

The woman lit up a cigarette and exhaled. 'Yes, and who would be coming for *this* place?'

Ten minutes later, they were all on their way, the bags receiving only a cursory glance from the long-awaited customs inspector.

Ellie leaned back in her seat. I am angry, she thought, and it's so close to the surface. The merest scratch and there it is. Anger at that woman, anger at Jean, at my mother, at all of this and everyone. All this darkness and anger, what do I do with it? How do I make it go away?

A narrow strip of blacktop parted low acacia woodland and unravelled past the bony, granite face of Longido, out onto open plains that flowed east to Kilimanjaro. The rains had failed here as well. Dust smoked up behind the Maasai cattle herds as small boys or old men in ragged shukas drove them onward toward imagined grazing. The earth tore open under their hooves.

Miles on, the town of Arusha began in clusters of bright blue or green painted buildings, then restaurants, schools, bill-boards for beer and cell phones. Closer in, there was traffic: Land Rovers, motorcycles, bicycles with ringing bells; carts pulled by wiry, sweating young men or by donkeys; goats, school children, women in bright kangas with bunches of green bananas balanced on their heads. It was a messy town, growing too fast like an adolescent teenager, and with the same tangled and confused energy. There was colour here, noise and music, mangoes, cassava, great gunnysacks of

266

beans, a shop selling pink and orange flip-flops.

Somewhere, Ellie hoped, among the fruit stands and the dusty back lanes, behind the mosque or the market, she would find Roy McMullen.

32

They entered a tunnel between sea and sky and came in low over the island. Ellie was misting the plane's window with her breath, drawing horses' heads. She dreamed of horses, of palominos and open fields — all means, Helen suspected, of escaping.

A small sign flapped in the wind on rusty hinges. 'Welcome to Islay.' Which Helen took as a bad joke because there was no welcome, only wind and low scrub and a car sent by the hotel with one headlight. Ellie skipped on the runway in her new pink dress. Helen thought, She looks like a bright bird, how light, how hollow-boned.

'Eleanor!' John said. 'Stop mucking about.'

He hadn't had his drink yet.

Ellie stopped abruptly, as if in a game of musical chairs.

★ ★ ★

'The Winslow Inn,' John said. 'More like the bloody Winds Blow Inn.' He and Helen actually managed a laugh. It was true, the wind slipped in between the window sashes and underneath the doors. Though why the wind, or anyone or anything, would want to enter these shabby rooms I cannot imagine, Helen thought. No care had been taken here. The brown carpet with lurid swirls. The bed with peeling varnish. The stained bath. An assortment of ashtrays purloined from other hotels: the Glasgow Intercontinental, the Fountain Inn, Malta. The Scots are so bloody cheap they'd stop breathing if they had to pay for air.

'I'll be in the pub,' John said.

Which was after all why they had come. This was John's pilgrimage. For here on this treeless, scrappy island off the west coast of Scotland was his favourite whisky made.

★   ★   ★

Helen and Ellie ate alone in the dining room because John was drinking. He was arranging with a man to go to the distillery tomorrow. His Lourdes, his Vatican. He was drinking silently with all the other silent drinkers in the silent, smoky pub in the dim glow of low-watt yellow light bulbs.

In the restaurant, piped music was playing.

'Mum,' Ellie said. 'Who is Kay Sir R?'

'It's Spanish. Que sera, sera. It means, 'Whatever will be, will be'.'

269

This was the song playing through what sounded like a tincan phone.

'Why?'

'It's about fate I suppose. How God or whoever has a plan for us.'

'Will I be rich?'

'I don't know.'

'Does God know?'

'I don't think God worries about those sorts of things. It's more important to be happy.'

'But you just said God has a plan for us.'

'I mean, maybe he just sets us on a course when we're very young and leaves it at that.'

'Will I be happy?'

'I hope so.'

'Are you happy, Mum?'

'Yes, of course I am. Now, hurry up. It's past your bedtime.'

They walked up the stairs. Helen was thinking about the song, the reassuring lyrics, sung by the wise older woman to the impetuous young girl. The future's not ours to see, whatever will be, will be. It suddenly seemed to Helen wicked, a wicked thing to say to a young girl: don't even try to direct your life, don't even imagine you will have a say in what happens to you. Surrender, forbear. Roll over and expose your pale belly in submission.

She put Ellie to bed, read her a story. As she sat there, watching her daughter fall asleep, touching the fine gold hairs on her daughter's arm, she realized she felt nothing.

Her love had simply worn out.

★ ★ ★

After midnight John stumbled in. He pulled off his trousers without first removing his shoes. He cursed and fell against the wall. There was more scuffling, the spilling of coins. Helen listened to one coin roll all the way across the floor and hit the skirting board by the window with a polite plink.

He came to bed still wearing his shirt, stinking of smoke and whisky. The bedsprings creaked. He pulled the covers over him, his back to her, and farted.

He dreamed.

And waking, trembled. 'Breathe,' she said, stroking his hair. 'It's okay, just take deep breaths.'

He shut his eyes tight and gritted his teeth.

'Don't leave me,' he said. 'Please don't leave me.'

'I'm here, I'm right here.'

She held him. Of course she held him.

★ ★ ★

They walked along the beach. An exhausted sea pushed and pulled at the pebbles. Ellie ran ahead, finding scallop shells, orange and pink, the only colour to be had.

An old man watched them pass. He saw a beautiful woman and her tall husband and her child who would wear nothing but her new pink dress. Helen imagined that the old man saw their solidarity, how they were a fort locked against the world.

John squeezed her closer. 'I'll stop.'

She looked ahead.

'When we get back.'

She remembered Berry Harrison at a lunch party, plying John with drink. 'Come on, old son, just one, just a weak one, you're past all that now. It's under control.'

'I'm going to call the Caldicotts and see if they're finally ready to sell,' he said. 'We just need a fresh start.'

Next week. Next month. Next year.

★　★　★

The pretty promises that light the way forward.

The Old Oak was as expected, dark and low-beamed, though Helen wondered about the name. Had there ever been an oak on Islay? Locals clustered around the bar and

272

did not look up or acknowledge the strangers among them.

The barman handed out menus. John ordered a double. Helen ordered the grilled trout. 'And fish and chips from your children's menu.'

'I don't want fish and chips,' Ellie said. She thumped her feet against the chair.

'Sweetheart, you love fish and chips,' said Helen.

'No, I don't.'

'Well, it's all they have for children.'

'I want chicken.' Thump, thump went Ellie's feet.

'There is no chicken.'

'I don't want fish and chips. I'll be sick.'

'Eleanor,' John said carefully.

Ellie looked back at him with bravery or insolence.

John ordered the poached trout and another whisky.

'I hate fish and chips!' Ellie said and slammed her feet into the table. The salt shaker teetered, John's whisky tipped and spilt. His hand flashed across the table to her face. The force propelled her back off her chair and onto the floor. Her head slammed against the leg of the table.

Helen reached down for her. Ellie's eyes were full of tears. But not terror. Already, there was a red welt rising on her cheek, Helen could see the outline of individual fingers. There was a bump the size of a robin's egg on the back of her head.

'Stop mucking about,' John said.

Everyone in The Old Oak had turned to look. Cigarettes and glasses were suspended in the air. Helen lifted Ellie to her feet and walked her to the ladies. She ran the tap and soaked a towel and washed her daughter's face.

'He didn't mean to hurt you. You know that. You know that.'

Ellie said nothing. Helen brushed her hair with her fingertips, the rough tangles only Rosa could extract. 'That's better.'

She took her compact out of her handbag and patted some powder on Ellie's cheeks. 'We'll have a nice lunch, okay, and you can have some custard for pudding. I saw it on the menu. You love custard.'

Ellie did not say: traitor, traitor. She said nothing.

Helen put her hands on Ellie's arms. 'I'm going to turn you around and when I do I'm going to see a big smile. I know there's a big, brave smile on the other side of you.'

But there was no smile. There were no tears.

Helen held Ellie's hand in her hers as they

walked back to the table, through the force field of disapproval. Helen wanted to yell at them: what are you looking at? You all hit your own children. Behind closed doors, with a belt or a hairbrush, their bottoms or their thighs, their backs, their faces too. Who do you think he learned it from?

But what she did was sit down. And Ellie sat down. John ordered another whisky, and they all ate their lunch.

33

The beggars had staked claim to the corners and sidestreets of Arusha. The women with snotty-nosed babies, the legless, the sightless, the crab-man, the leper. Here, on display, was everything that could go horribly wrong with the human body. A man on a hand-wheel bike with elephant legs. A child with disease-swollen eyes. They took their places patiently among the bead and batik sellers, the safari touts and the hawkers of fruit, secondhand newspapers, postcards. Everyone was selling something, from pity to the Serengeti, and they tried to sell it all to Ellie as she walked to the post office.

She had written a polite note to Roy McMullen. Do you remember me? It's about my father, some questions. Could we meet at your convenience? I am staying at the Swara Guest House. She posted the letter.

A restless posse of street boys were waiting for her.

'Mother, mother give me money, give me money,' they chanted.

A woman held up her crying baby, a man with milky eyes smiled and held out a tin cup.

Ellie escaped past them, through them, and into a small café. What do you do, she wanted to know. Do you empty your purse, throw all your money on the pavement? Steal a butter giraffe from the hotel buffet? She suddenly understood why people blocked the great tide of despair with high walls and security guards, rolled up their windows and blasted the air conditioning. It was a kind of defence. Nothing I do will be enough so I won't do anything at all.

She thought of Peter, who slept in bed as if flung across the universe. What would he do, she wondered, confronted by this misery? He would tell her to give her father's money away. What could she ever use it for herself? Just give it back, here, where it belongs. He would talk about structure and material, about shelter, roofs, floors, stairways and windows, about light. He would draw plans for schools and clinics on bar napkins with leaky pens. He would say, 'The changes you could make, Ellie, the good things, in a big way, a real way, not just dimes or shillings, not just spare change or sympathy or nice tips.'

And Peter knew about tips. He was, after all, the last of the great tippers. Which was how they had met, because she got his whole order wrong when he came into the restaurant on a busy Saturday night and he left her ten bucks on top of a twenty-dollar tab.

She had followed him out to the parking lot. 'I can't take it. I gave you lousy service.'

'So what?'

'A tip is supposed to be for good service. This is like a proposition or something.'

He had laughed. 'I left you ten bucks not a thousand. Now that would have been a proposition.'

He had been looking at her in that late-summer light with the low-riders cruising by on El Paseo and the hermanos cranking the boom-boom bass in their pickups. Even now she could remember that moment exactly. And how he would hold her hand when crossing the street. And how he refused to cut the grass in his garden, despite the snippy notes from neighbours reminding him of town bylaws, because the creatures that lived there, the birds and snakes and squirrels, seemed to like the long grass and overgrown bushes. She knew that all her life she'd look for him in airports and train stations, on streets; she'd see glimpses of him in other men, the turn of a head, a gesture of hands, his fineness, his decency.

★   ★   ★

As she stepped back onto the street she saw the motorcycle and the man from the border.

He smiled, 'I remember you.'

'Sorry about that,' she said. 'I was just angry at her.'

'Sorry, Jesus. I thought what you said was great.' He moved onto the sidewalk. Nearer, he was taller than she expected. 'How about coffee?'

'Thanks. I just had one.'

'Tea?'

'I have to go.'

'Are you from here?'

'No,' she said and saw a smudge of oil or soot on his cheek near his ear. She thought of inky, blue smudges. 'Not really. Maybe a long time ago.'

'Look,' he said. 'If you've got a few hours, come with me, this place east of town. No one really knows about it. But I know you'd like it.'

For a moment she thought to ask about Roy McMullen — did he know of him? But then there would be other questions, explanations. And she thought she'd say no, because she had been here before with other men. Because she saw the gold band on his left ring finger. She knew very well how it started: like this. And how it ended: in the morning or in a week, when one of them walked away.

She didn't quite nod but he understood and turned to the bike and started the engine.

34

On their last day on Islay, Helen woke early. The floorboards creaked underfoot as she walked to the basin in the corner and washed her face. Looking in the mirror, she touched the lines at the corner of her eyes, tried to smooth away the ones on her forehead. She was thirty-five. One day she would be an old woman and John would be dead. He'd have left her his money and she would be free to live as she wanted. But by then, what would be left to want? Maybe to go back in time and break every whisky bottle.

I am a kind of alcoholic, she thought, just like him. I do everything and I do nothing in deference to the Lord God Whisky. Every compromise, every lie, every broken promise. I might as well be doing the drinking.

She opened the door and went out into the narrow dark hallway. She had almost reached the stairway when she felt Ellie's hand reaching for hers. Her daughter could float above the floor, could move silently through space. Her daughter heard everything but made no sound herself. She even spoke in whispers so as not to wake the beast.

'Can I come?'

'If you'd like.'

'Where are you going?'

'I don't know really. Just a walk.'

Ellie was barefoot and put her shoes on only when she had reached the safety of the stairway.

They walked along the stony beach, toward the headland, bracing against the cold wind and the damp air. They took a narrow path through tawny scrub and tussocky grass. Sharp-winged terns flew above them and there were great flocks of seagulls further out, looming and skimming the pewter surface of the sea. A distant squall cornered what little there was of the sun.

The wind came up as they rounded a cove, and there were rafts of sea mist. Here the earth tilted upward and broke off into slabs of cliff and rough rock. The path petered out, but they kept on, climbing higher to reach the apex of the island. Helen felt like a sailor desperately trying to sight land, some other land, anywhere but here.

Her hair came loose from its scarf, or maybe she let it loose, her dark hair swirling around her head, and she was suddenly walking faster.

'Wait!' Ellie said.

But Helen wasn't listening or waiting. She was running uphill.

35

She lets go of your hand. You run, trying to keep up. Where is she going? There is nowhere to go, only more island. There is no path. She keeps going, pushing through the bushes and up the hill. She is running. The bushes catch at your clothes and tear your new pink dress. You think of the children on Bizarre Street grabbing at you with their sticky fingers.

Then Mum is too far ahead. You yell out, 'Wait!' But the wind throws your voice away. You are tangled in the bushes and you stumble on the rocks. Your knee is bleeding and you can't see her anymore. You shout and shout but she doesn't come back.

The wind is screaming like a kettle. It is trying to lift your skin from your bones, your hair from your head. You look back and cannot see the town. Or even the path back. Everything has run away from you. Even Mum. There is only white cloud and the sea somewhere below.

You will never be able to remember how far you walked in the mist, maybe only minutes, maybe hours, before you see her again.

She is standing on an arm of land that goes out high over the sea. She is in the rain and the wind, on tiptoes it seems, about to keep walking, only she has run out of land. The sea below is shouting up at her.

'Mum!' You want her to hear you so you stand at the edge of the cliff. You shout louder than the sea. 'Mum!'

She turns. She is saying something to you but you cannot hear. Her mouth is open and her hair is snapping and snarling in the wind. She is running at you and she grabs you from behind and the two of you fall back into the scratchy bushes and grass. She is shaking you.

'Stupid girl! Stupid child!'

She holds you to her then.

'You could have fallen. The cliff. You could have been killed.'

Holding you so close you cannot breathe. She is crying.

'I'm sorry. I'm so sorry,' she is saying.

But you are moving away from her. You are leaving her. She has only your body. You are flying above her with the screaming birds. You are looking down on the slatey sea and Mum kneeling on the edge of the cliff saying, 'My little girl, my little girl, I'm so sorry.'

36

Pat O'Shea was one of the few whites who'd stayed on in the police force after independence, an overweight redhead with pasty, sweating skin. He had a reputation as a brutal little shit. Which was why the Government kept him on. He knew how to interrogate and how to terrify, how to get answers to questions, not just answers to stop the pain. Berry Harrison knew all about Pat O'Shea and his talent. He told Helen, trying to impress her: 'Forget flying planes and running businesses, these munts are lining up to learn how to torture. But it's a technique, a skill. They'll muck it up the way they muck everything else up.' Helen thought to ask, 'Just how do you muck up torture, Berry? Are there dead bodies instead of mutilated ones? Or is it the other way around?'

She really didn't like Berry, maybe she even hated Berry. But hating was a luxury she couldn't afford in the little world of Nairobi. It was pointless besides, for there were Berrys everywhere; lowborn kings and queens who strutted and pouted. Helen wore lovely dresses and laughed among them, laughed at their jokes because she hadn't the courage to do otherwise. What do you call an African virgin? A pre-dickie-munt. What do you call an African chef? Condi-munt. Helen always pretended she didn't hear.

But she heard what Berry was saying about Pat O'Shea. You wouldn't have him in your house for a social occasion, God no, wretched little man, but you called him if you suspected your houseboy of stealing and wanted to scare the sugar out of him. Or if you needed a little white magic: background information on a potential business partner, compromising photographs, that sort of thing. Helen let herself be impressed and let Berry's hand move up her thigh to the hem of her pretty dress.

The next day she rang the main police switchboard and asked for Patrick O'Shea. After a moment, he came on the line. She said, 'My name is Helen Cameron. I need to speak with you about a private matter.'

He told her to meet him at the Karimji Curry House on the Athi Road. 'Out of town, away from peepers.'

She wanted to laugh: he sounded so *noir*.

The Karimji Curry House looked exactly like the kind of place you'd meet for an illicit assignation. Past the tyre factory and the turn-off for the airport, it was stuck behind a

Caltex petrol station. So many cars were coming and going that if yours was spotted you had the excuse of a flat tyre or battery. Inside, the walls were gold, but tacky with dust and grease. There was a strong stink of ghee and cardamom. She remembered that smell, and those years ago in Kampala when she had been someone else, the slanted, lemon light in Henry's courtyard and the fat Indian women in their spice-coloured saris.

There were no customers in the Karimji Curry House. Helen was sure it was a front for God knew what, ivory smuggling, the white slave trade, drugs, whatever was coming through Nairobi to or from the thousands of smugglers' coves along the coast.

She waited only a few minutes before O'Shea arrived. He was an ugly man with a smug look. Right away she didn't like him. But she wasn't here to like him.

He sat down. 'Mrs Cameron, how can I help you?'

'My husband is having an affair,' she said.

Pat O'Shea nodded. She felt his little piggy eyes appraising her, judging her: what are you lacking that your husband looks to another woman? 'And why do you think this?'

'I know.'

'The famous woman's intuition.'

'It's not intuition, it's obvious.'

'You want a divorce?'

'Yes.'

O'Shea shrugged. 'You need a lawyer.'

'I've been to a lawyer, Mr O'Shea.'

'Sergeant.'

'Sergeant. He won't help. That's why I'm here with you.'

Helen recalled Richard Boudreau and how he'd sat there and told her she couldn't just ask for a divorce as one might ask for a new hat. There must be fault, there must be reason. Surely things aren't so bad, he had said. I know your husband, Mrs Cameron, he's a good provider.

He drinks, he hits our daughter, Helen had said.

A tipple every now and then. A little discipline, that's all. Boudreau had even smiled. Difficult to prove abuse, he had said, unless there are hospital bills and witnesses. Are things that bad?

No, she had said.

And I must ask, Mrs Cameron, if you have any means of support should you leave John? Family money? A job? A five-year separation is required before a contested divorce — and I'm assuming he would contest. Could you provide for yourself and the child during that time?

Helen had said, 'What about adultery?'

Boudreau had tilted his head to the side, 'Then things might be in your favour.'

'I've been to a lawyer,' Helen said now to O'Shea. 'That's why I'm here.'

O'Shea said, 'Adultery can be tricky to prove. I'd need pictures, statements, you'll have to name the correspondent.'

'When I have the proof that's her problem, his problem.'

'He's had other affairs?'

'I don't think so.'

'How long has it been going on for?'

'Six months, I think. It started after we got back from a holiday in Scotland.'

'Why not ignore it this time? Maybe you can talk it through.'

She looked at him. 'I want to leave him.'

'Of course, I understand how important the alimony must be for someone like you.'

Helen's mouth opened and shut. She stood abruptly and started away from the table.

'It's all right, Mrs Cameron. Don't get your knickers in a twist.' He knew they all had to get up and try and walk out when he said things like that. Had to prove to him — and themselves — that morality or love or selfhood was the issue here, not money.

She turned back to him. He patted the table. 'Come on, tell me about it.' She told him everything she knew. How on Wednesday and Friday afternoons she had her flower arranging class and her French cooking class. And that's when it happened. Eileen and John. Sometimes in her house, but maybe also in a hotel. John was never in the office on those afternoons.

O'Shea made a few notes and told her his fee was two hundred pounds.

Helen paid him cash. She'd been shaving money off the grocery bill, fudging the numbers. It was only a matter of time before John would notice.

O'Shea shook Helen's hand, 'It's a done deal. Don't you worry about a thing, Mrs Cameron.'

Driving back into Nairobi Helen suddenly felt high. She was going to do this. After all these years she was going to leave John. She saw herself living back in England in a village like the one in which she grew up. She'd buy a nice little cottage for herself and Ellie — he could afford it. Ellie would go to the local school and Helen could become a gardener. And a cook. She would make relishes with the vegetables she grew and jams with berries she picked in the woods. She would sew dresses for Ellie and knit sweaters for the cold winters.

She looked out the windshield at the

Ngongs in the west. Those five ridges anchored the whole landscape. Without them, Nairobi would be a marsh in a dull, barren plain.

37

The motorcycle was heading east on a newly tarred road, through roadside villages of women selling blue buckets of red tomatoes, past coffee farms and banana groves, under looming shade trees. When they drove under the trees, the temperature dropped to a chill so that the sun ahead offered warm relief. He was a good driver and Ellie felt safe tucked behind him on the bike, her hands holding his waist but not too tightly. Not intimately.

After an hour, they turned right onto a rough dirt track. There were now no other cars, only women on foot walking with jerry cans of water on their heads, or girls carrying bundles of hay, or serious men on bicycles. They passed a small boy on a large bicycle. He rode canted to one side, his legs under the crossbar instead of astride it, his arms stretching to the handlebars. On the back was a goat trussed into a reed basket.

There was a maze of tracks to be negotiated, a scattering of huts where ragged children squatted in the dust with toys homemade from cans and wood and scavenged plastic. And then one last burst of open ground before a welling of palms and fig trees.

They got off the bike. He took her hand and led her into the trees. She did not expect to see an oasis, and he smiled when he saw her wonder at the deep clear pool among the tree roots and palm fronds.

'It's a spring,' he told her. 'They think it comes from the mountain, from Kilimanjaro. But it's warm, so it must come from inside the mountain.'

She crouched down and put her hand in the water. It was impossibly clear and she could see grains of fine sand and small stones ten feet down.

'You can swim if you like,' he said. 'There aren't any crocs. Only further up the river, but they never come here.'

She pulled off her T-shirt and jeans, hesitating with her underwear. And then she took that off, too, for she didn't care, and neither did he. She felt there was a pact between them: somehow they needed the same thing and it wasn't sex.

They swam for a while and then lay out on the flat rocks in the sun beyond the pool. Birds flew overhead or sounded in the trees. He knew their names. Egret, ibis, hornbill, kingfisher.

'I'm sorry,' he said.

'Why?' She looked at him over the crook of her arm.

'I sound like a tour guide. I can't turn it off.'

'Is that what you do?'

He nodded. 'I wonder when I crossed the line from being able to just look at things and allowing them to be, to now when I have to name them and know their diets and their habits and where I can find them.'

'Does it matter? The birds are there either way.'

'How can I explain it — it's wanting to also be somehow nameless instead of who I've become, this safari guide, with this predictable life, where I go, what I tell my clients, the same stories around the campfire. I exist as a kind of fantasy figure, what people imagine they'll find when they come on safari here. Even my wife — ' He stopped himself.

'It's okay,' she said. 'I don't even know your name.'

He turned to her and reached out and put his hand on the side of her face. She put hers over it.

'Even my wife didn't marry *me*, but someone she imagined me to be.'

She was the daughter of a wealthy client, he said, a beautiful French girl who loved Africa, or thought she did. They had two children and a house with servants and horses, but now she wanted to move back to France. She'd had enough of the dust and the flies, she wanted real cheese, fresh brioche, winter, education for the children, telephones that worked.

'Some other Africa,' Ellie said.

'And who *would* want this one?'

'You do.'

'Because it's all I know.'

'Because it's a real place. You know it as a real place.'

He withdrew his hand and rolled onto his back. He told her about the years of socialism in Tanzania after independence, the forced agriculturalization of teachers and other 'intellectuals'. They were made to leave the cities and towns, given plots of land and hoes, and told to farm. There was starvation and despair, he said. There were years when it was impossible to buy toothpaste or cigarettes, when flour and sugar were luxuries. His family had clung to their coffee farm in the south, paying bribes to keep their land, living like Africans on scrawny chickens and wild spinach. They *were* Africans — the English, Dutch and German had long ago evaporated from their blood.

'I remember being old enough to smoke,' he said. 'Fourteen or so, and I'd go to the local bar and there was a guy there, you know the city-slicker type with attitude and purple flared trousers and cheap Chinese sunglasses. So cool, so hip even though he'd probably never gone further than Morogoro. And he would sell puffs of his cigarettes. The cigarette was on a pin and he'd hand it round. About ten of us would be smoking one cigarette, paying for each puff. It's funny because what we felt wasn't deprivation or humiliation but an incredible sense of camaraderie. White or black, Chaga or Mpare or Maasai or Mzungu, we belonged to this country. It was our country, and the mistakes were our mistakes, and we made them honestly, with integrity.'

'And now? Has that changed?'

He waited for a while, seeming to watch the afternoon sky deepen toward evening. 'How could I ever move to France? And yet how can I not? How can I say I love a country more than my wife and children?'

Above them, the ibises came drifting home to roost in the fig trees. Ellie thought of the landscapes they carried in them, the sufficiency of their lives. She thought of the man beside her whose sense of belonging was a curse. He would drive her back to her guesthouse in Arusha and she would never see him again. They both understood that secrets are safest with strangers.

Peter had said she hoarded secrets, that she used them as a kind of weapon against him. He was right, she saw now, but weapons of defence and not attack. His love had surrounded her like a siege and she had felt she could not control what was freely given and what was taken.

38

Helen met O'Shea in the parking lot of a small church in Kiambu, their cars parked together bumper to hood so they could speak through their driver's side windows. It had been a month since they'd met in the Karimji Curry House.

He said: 'Your husband's not having an affair, Mrs Cameron.'

She looked at him. 'Of course he is. With Eileen McMullen.'

'I couldn't find any evidence of it.'

'Did you try?'

He gave her a warning look. 'Maybe it's over between them. I'm not saying you're wrong. I'm saying there's no proof. It ain't happening now.'

'Ain't', she thought. How ridiculous.

Turning ahead, she stared out the windshield at the small graveyard behind the church. She remembered that John's father was buried here. She and John had come once, years ago now, to lay some flowers. The graves were untended and overrun with weeds.

'Thank you anyway,' she said. She was

polite, careful not to dismiss. Manners were a mask, not to preserve his feelings but hers. She would not allow him the pleasure of her disappointment.

'If I can be of assistance in the future, please don't hesitate to contact me,' he said.

She studied him for a moment. His balloon-shaped head, his watercolour skin. What had he lost that had made him as he was? Because it's the loss that shapes us, never the gain. The amputations, the thefts.

He drove away in his battered Land Rover and she thought: He's lying, he's a lying bastard. But why? Why has he lied?

★   ★   ★

On the way home she stopped by the dukha to pick up a grocery order. The store was crammed with tins and boxes, much of it imported. Mr Abdulla knew his British clients wanted Marmite and chocolate and soft toilet paper. He was always cheerful, a tall slim man in a white robe, an embroidered fez on his bald head. The tassel jiggled when he laughed. But when he met her today he was quiet, eyes down, and at first Helen thought he must be ill.

'How are you, Mr Abdulla?' she said.

He forced his smile then slid his eyes

sideways along the counter. 'Your account has been closed, madame. Pardon me,' he said. 'As of today.'

She almost laughed as she glimpsed the corner of Pat O'Shea's lie like a petticoat.

'My husband rang you, did he?' she said.

Mr Abdulla wiped invisible dust from the counter. 'I'm so very sorry, madame, very sorry.' His wife sat at the far end of the counter, knitting. For years Helen hadn't noticed her there. She was dressed like a shadow in her black bui-bui and she never moved or spoke, apart from flicking the needles through some lurid pink or yellow wool. But today she lifted her coffee-bean eyes and looked at Helen with scorn. Yes, Helen was sure it was scorn, as if she was saying, 'Now you know you are no different to me, despite your white skin and your bare arms.'

Helen met those eyes again as she turned to leave the shop. She saw the resentment but also a fierce and private strength. Mrs Abdulla had long ago left her husband and built her own world, self-reliant and independent behind that black veil.

★ ★ ★

In the evening, John said nothing about Mr Abdulla, so neither did Helen. At dinner, she divulged some neighbourhood gossip; the Americans were leaving, the Swiss had renewed their contract for another three years, the Richardses had separated. She made sure he drank enough.

After he had gone to bed she looked in his briefcase and found his chequebook. The day before he'd written a cheque for cash for four hundred pounds.

She imagined O'Shea strutting up to John's office, 'I know something you don't, pal.' Strutting so everyone could see the gun on his hip. 'It'll cost you two hundred.'

John would want to know. About what? My wife? My business partners?

'Your wife. Two hundred for the details.'

And when O'Shea had the money in his grubby little hands, he said, 'She wants the goods on you. She knows you're having an affair. She wants divorce, she wants alimony.'

Maybe he even had photographs. John and Eileen, their needs colliding on Wednesday afternoons. Maybe he showed them to John.

'And it'll cost you another two for me to tell her you ain't having an affair, to lose these lovely snapshots.'

John paid, of course he paid. And then he phoned Mr Abdulla's Grocery and Market

Shop. It was a warning, a reminder to Helen. Don't leave me. A command, not a plea.

At breakfast, she said: 'There's a problem with the account at Abdulla's.'

He looked at her. But she was so good at pretending now. He saw her smooth, beautiful face half-turned toward him. She was returning to him. 'Oh, I'll phone him today and clear it up,' he said.

★　★　★

And then, a week later, she was home from her cooking class. She parked the car and turned the engine off, and Ellie came running to say, Mrs McMullen is dead.

Helen went directly along the path through the hedge, into the house, a house like hers, already abandoned, the inhabitants only pretending to live there, squatters, vagrants. She went up the stairs to the bedroom. John had been there, she could smell him, his aftershave, and the way he disturbed the air, if that could be so, the handprint his being left behind. Eileen was dead. A faded, sad beauty slumped against the sink with the cord of her dressing gown around her neck.

But Helen was too intent to care. She was looking around, on the bed, the dressing table.

A hysteric like Eileen would leave a note. A note that named John, blamed him. A note Helen could show the judge: here, this is the man I want to leave. See, he is named by his mistress who killed herself.

But there was only a used condom in the wastebasket. Could she present that to the judge? Here, Your Honour, Exhibit A: this is what infidelity looks like.

Why was there no note? Who had taken it? Had John come back and found her and taken the note? Or had Baptist or Rosa, unable to read, afraid that the note might implicate them, hidden it, thrown it away?

The note was all she had needed to leave John. She sat down on the edge of the bath and bowed her head in obedience.

When Roy came he found her crying. He thought it was because of Eileen.

39

Ellie stepped out of the guesthouse and past the captive birds penned on the small front lawn. The flamingos were stretching, wings flexing and ruffling, unfolding their long paper-clip legs. They seemed unconcerned by their captivity; they had each other, food, shade, sun. The blazing landscape of Lake Nakuru or Manyara, the freedom of flight and clarity of altitude were lost to them, no more than a dream — or less: the loosened hem of memory, fraying into oblivion. The spoonbill squawked and plodded toward its tiny pond.

There had been no reply from Roy for a week, and Ellie could find no trace of him in the phone book or anywhere else she could think to ask, the hospital, the Greek Club, the Gymkhana Club. She had walked Arusha's streets and avenues, buffeted by the chaos of the town, the blasting horns of minibuses crammed with people, the creeping despair of the flower seller whose unsold roses wilted in the late afternoon sun. She had drunk coffee and tea and read out-of-date newspapers. She knew everything that had happened in the world last week. She had lain awake at night listening to the banana leaves tussle in the dry wind and the backpacking couple next door making love. She wrote no postcards. Who to?

But today she went to the Post Office, to the counter marked Enquiries. She said, 'I'm trying to find Dr Roy McMullen. His box number is 15274.'

The man behind the counter suggested she write a letter.

'I did,' she said. 'I was hoping you might have some further record. Perhaps a street address, a telephone number.'

'There is this information,' the man said. 'But it is not for public.'

So Ellie went outside and put ten thousand shillings in an envelope and went back into the Post Office and gave it to the man. She thought, this is how I begin, in this small and insignificant way. Five hundred through a gate, ten thousand in an envelope. The poetry everyone whispers on this continent. And my father, the Laureate.

★ ★ ★

She did not look at the map. She simply followed directions. Take a bus to Mto wa Mbu. Ask there for rides to Gelai. There are no taxis to Gelai, there is not even a real road

306

to Gelai. She took the bus, leaving Arusha and anything resembling a paved road and a cold drink. The bus creaked and crabbed at full tilt, the axles held together with baling twine or clothes pins, the driver chewing myrah and throwing the stems out the window.

At Mto wa Mbu, beneath the heavy fig trees, she found her ride, a Land Rover pick up. She paid extra for the front seat, which she shared with two others beside the driver. At the last moment, she was handed a small boy named Goodluck, who sat on her lap. In the back, meanwhile, an extraordinary number of Maasai had packed themselves in vertically, like toothpicks. Someone tied three large bunches of green bananas to the roof and a goat found some space among the Maasai.

★ ★ ★

They skirted the Ngorongoro highlands, those high, green volcanic cliffs embraced above with rainforest and cloud. They passed through villages, the first with cement buildings and tin roofs, but then only rough mud and thatch. Further out, fewer people wore shoes, their clothes ever more ragged. The shambas also became less ambitious, the ploughed earth a tentative parting of the high grass and scrub.

And then there were no more farms. Wide plains of yellow grass rose into soft hills and the dust-padded light made distance uncertain. Ellie saw giraffe floating like yachts through the afternoon heat. There were herds of Maasai cattle and zebra in the long grass. Time was nothing more than the bumpy road, the jolting tyres, the film of dust on her face. Goodluck fell asleep on her lap and she let her hand caress the tight, black curls of his head.

Civilization was behind them now. Ellie felt a certain release, as if her body were equalizing under pressure. She had never been this far out, this far away. Even in the depths of New Mexico or Utah there was always the presence of man, a plane, a power line — some reminder of how humankind had claimed the land. But here, the hills and plains, the high ridge of Ngorongoro, seemed to defy intervention. She could almost believe that man's only mark on the planet was this track, eddying into the wild under an unblinking sky.

By nightfall, Gelai was visible — a string of lights across a black hillside, the only lights but for the stars. They broached the distance in the pitch dark. Closer, she could hear the thump of a single generator, laughter, a radio. Darkness brought them into the village, among the mud shacks and the Maasai. A goat stood on a dead car and shook the bell around its neck, as if heralding her here, to the end of the earth.

★   ★   ★

The villagers stared at her as if she had landed from outer space. She could see the whites of their eyes and the whiteness of their teeth in the lamp glow. Their slim bodies fused with the darkness. They wore beads at their necks, ankles and wrists, their shoes were made from old car tyres and they carried spears which they knew how to use. They smelled of earth and cow, and they beheld her silently. She had Goodluck with her, cocked on one hip. She had grown accustomed to the drowsy weight of him.

'Ninataka ongea na Doctor McMullen,' she said.

There were nods, a murmur. One, a moran, a young warrior, stepped forward. 'Come, come.'

He led her past a row of shacks and small shops selling packets of detergent, cigarettes and warm Coke. Beyond the shops, there was little light. She walked close to the moran and her eyes adjusted so she could see quite clearly the world laid out in starlight. The volcanic cone of Lengai, Lake Natron's shallow stillness, the Gol Mountains, Olkarien, Olduvai, Empakai.

Some other Africa, she thought. It is here after all.

Up ahead there were white stones marking an entrance and a light in the window of a white building. A small sign: 'Gelai Medical Clinic'. The moran smiled and nodded. 'Dokta Roy.' They walked to the building, up onto the small veranda. The moran knocked softly on the door. They waited. The door opened.

She recognized him and was surprised by how little he had changed. Smaller, shorter now than her. But his hair still rose upward of its own accord into a peak, only now it was white. He was slighter, there was the start of a stoop. He wore a faded Oxford shirt, old khakis and flip-flops.

He raised his eyebrows, looking from Ellie to the child. He opened the door completely. 'How can I help? The boy, is it?'

'No,' she said. 'I don't know who he belongs to. He's just sleepy. We came from Mto wa Mbu.'

Roy spoke to the moran in Kimaa. There was an answer. 'Someone has gone to get his mother,' Roy said. 'She'll come soon. Meanwhile, come in. We can put him on the sofa.'

They entered a small clean room bordered by benches, chairs and a sofa. There were posters on the wall in Swahili warning of AIDS, recommending that mothers breast feed, urging the boiling of cow's milk. Ellie carefully placed Goodluck on the sofa. Roy brought a crocheted blanket from somewhere and put it over him.

'Now,' he said, looking at her. 'You've been travelling. Would you like some tea? I'm sorry I can't offer you a beer or anything stronger.'

'Tea would be great.'

★   ★   ★

He took her through the clinic to his own quarters and onto another veranda. The sparseness made her think of a mission. But there were no crucifixes lurking, no bibles, no pictures of a blond-haired, blue-eyed Jesus. She glimpsed a bedroom, neatly kept, a small bathroom and kitchen. Only a bookshelf filled with Dick Francis novels gave a clue to the long hours Roy kept for himself.

He lit another kerosene lamp and placed the tea between them on a small wooden table. They sat on old canvas chairs. Beyond the veranda Ellie could make out a high euphorbia hedge and the view directly to Lengai.

'I'm Ellie,' she said. 'Eleanor Cameron.'

'I thought you must be.'

'You got my letter?'

'A few days ago. It came with some supplies.' He looked at her. 'I'm sorry I didn't reply. I was going to. Time is different out here.' He laughed. 'There's an old colonial saying, 'We've got the watches and they've got the time.' Well, I don't have a watch anymore. Haven't for years. Looked at the calendar the other day and realized I was off by two years.'

'I hope it's not an imposition. Just turning up like this.'

'Not at all. There's a spare bed. Stay as long as you like. I'm just not sure how much I can help you. It's been so many years. Memory is a notoriously unreliable witness. And John — ' he gave a shrug of his thin shoulders, 'John was an elusive man.'

So this would be his excuse, his abdication: the failure of memory. And when she spoke, the words came out in a rush and she could not keep the desperation from her voice. 'I have all these questions, all these pieces.'

Roy saw her eyes quicken away from him, how she tried to hide what she felt, clumsily, like a child. He knew pain when he saw it. He leaned in, toward her. 'Ask me,' he said gently. 'I'll tell you what I know.'

★   ★   ★

'What happened to Nina?'

Roy exhaled softly. 'She died. Of pneumonia. She was thirteen or fourteen. Very incapacitated by that point. She became very ill and her doctor and I just agreed to let her go.'

'Before. To begin with.'

'Her umbilical cord caught round her neck during birth. She was deprived of oxygen. There was permanent brain damage.'

Ellie thought back. Nina in her nappies, screaming her protest at the unjustness of it all. 'I never knew what it was,' she said. 'I'm so sorry.'

'For Eileen, for Nina. Not for me. I am still here. And, mostly, happy.'

Ellie looked at his old face. She wondered at the choices that had brought him here.

'Mrs McMullen — Eileen — she was having an affair with my father.'

'You knew?'

'I saw them once.'

'And your mother, did she know?'

'I've no idea. We've never talked about it. About any of it.'

Roy waited for a moment. 'I was a doctor, I should have tried harder to have empathy with what Eileen was going through. She was severely depressed, but I felt only relief that it took her further and further away from me. Eventually, we — I — had to send Nina back to England. She needed care we couldn't get for her in Kenya. But it broke Eileen. At the time I just thought I was doing what was necessary, but I think I also wanted to hurt her.'

And this was his exile, his penance. Ellie understood: Of all that had gone from Roy McMullen, his guilt remained. It clung like a burr to his heart. How cruel and selfish he had been. How reckless.

He went on. 'Eileen and John, it wasn't much of an affair, I don't think. They were both such damaged people. Perhaps it was something physical. Maybe they just needed each other. I think he tried to end it. And then, well, she — not because of him, but I think she'd just reached the end. But you know that, you found the body.'

There was nothing beyond the lamplight, the darkness of the edge of the world existed beyond the horizon.

Ellie said, 'No. My father killed her.'

For a long moment Roy said nothing. She thought he was considering this, the shock of it, the sense of it.

'Have you always believed this?' He turned to her.

'There had been an argument. They had been fighting.'

'Ellie,' he said, and she knew from his tone of voice that he was trying to stop her.

'No.' She held up the word like a shield. 'They had been fighting, Baptist heard them, they had just been together in your bed.'

Roy was looking at her, and then away.

'I'd seen them before, he was violent toward her.' Ellie felt the hot night air, the sweat at the back of her neck. 'He killed her. Why can't you see that? Why does everyone want to believe he was innocent? You of all people. She was your wife!'

'Ellie, it's all about ligatures. I saw for myself. The ligatures on her neck went up behind her ears, not horizontally across her throat as in strangulation. She put one end of the sash around her neck, the other over the door and tied it to the door handle, and then she very deliberately hung herself with the weight of her own body.'

Ellie stood, pushed the chair away and walked to the edge of the light. She knew the truth, her truth: this was one thing that would not be left behind or taken from her.

Roy said: 'There was so much going on

that you couldn't have known about. You were a child. Things were kept from you. Ellie, there was a policeman, a mzungu, I've forgotten his name, who tried to blackmail your father. He knew about the affair. He had proof. He said he'd give it to Helen. He knew everything about your father, whatever there was to know — there may have been other women but it was the bank accounts outside the country that were his real leverage. The money laundering was illegal and the World Bank was pressuring the Kenyan Government to crack down. They would have been more than happy to make an example of your father. O'Shea — that was his name, could have handed John to them on a platter.

'That was the joke, you see. O'Shea was who we all went to when we needed something fixed, when we needed to make a problem disappear — or appear. But he had files on all of us. If he ran short of cash he just showed up on your doorstep with your file. Your father paid. I don't know how much. Enough.'

'Maria Riktoffen was strangled.' Ellie turned to Roy. 'She was my father's lover at the time of her death. That is what Pat O'Shea found out about my father.'

'Maria? Why on earth would John kill her?'

'He was a violent man. Maybe he didn't

mean to. That was always the excuse, 'He didn't mean to.' And so the pain he caused didn't mean anything either.'

Roy came and stood beside her. 'It must have been so lonely for you in that house.'

She was aware of the weakness in her voice, the breaking apart of syllables. 'That's not it at all. O'Shea found out the truth,' she said, insisting. 'About Maria, about Eileen. My father just paid his way out of it. He's even paid me.'

His hand was on her shoulder. 'He paid for O'Shea's silence. Because he knew Helen was trying to leave him. That she'd take you. He was desperate, not guilty. He didn't want to lose his wife and child. You were all he had.'

Ellie said nothing, had nothing to say. She felt that if she stepped out of the narrow circle of light that bound her to this house and this old man she would vanish in the darkness, she would dissolve.

40

It was afternoon. Helen was sitting at her desk doing the month's accounts. John was having a nap, Ellie was playing in the garden. The phone bill, the water bill, the servants' salaries. How neatly everything tallied. She stapled the receipts to the page. She double-checked her figures. The numbers obeyed her. Was this why John had chosen accountancy? For the order, the neatness, which in everything else was impossible?

When she reached into the top drawer for a paperclip, she saw the two passports. Two black books, barely used, hers and Ellie's, subjects of Her Majesty. She put them in her bag and stood up.

It wasn't courage, she wasn't brave. She didn't even close the desk drawer.

She had no money, just what was in her bag.

Rosa was ironing clothes behind the kitchen.

'I'm leaving,' Helen said to her.

'You come back what time?'

'No. This house, the bwana. Ellie and I are going.'

Rosa said nothing.

Helen reached out and touched her arm. It still amazed her, the difference between black and white skin. 'I'll send for you when I have some money.'

'Where?'

'I don't know,' Helen said.

Rosa nodded. 'Pole.' Sorry for you. Be careful.

Helen reminded herself, they work for you, you owe them only their salaries. But it wasn't true. Rosa's kindness hadn't been paid for, neither had her love for Ellie.

'You've been a good friend to me,' she said. 'Thank you.'

Rosa kept folding the sheets. 'Take care of the toto.'

Then Helen broke away, walking quickly to the garden. Ellie was in her sandpit.

Helen said. 'Come with me, sweetheart.'

'Why?' Ellie looked up at her.

'I'll explain everything later.'

'Where are we going?'

'Please, just come now. We have to hurry.'

As they walked toward the car, Helen glanced up at the bedroom window. John was watching them. She squeezed Ellie's hand and said, 'Run.'

41

She waited until dawn. She walked into the gold world while the shadows still slept furled against the hills and mountains around Gelai. It was all she could do, to repeat the pattern of her whole life, to walk away. Walking, she did not have to think or feel. There was only direction, movement. The co-ordinates of her destination were uncertain. But her heart was a compass.

A jackal trotted across her path and further on she saw a herd of zebra wading across the plains. The topography was such that she did not seem to be leaving Gelai. The mountains ahead and the village behind remained the same distance.

The horizon absorbed miles and time.

She walked on. The pale salt-starched earth compressed beneath her feet, the sharp alkaline tang of the air prickled with the sweat on her skin. The heat clung to her as if animate, with the weight and breath of a beast. With its great arms around her, she found it difficult to breathe. She staggered.

Mirages appeared: animals became trees, villages liquefied. The landscape shape-shifted around her, became uncertain as in a dream. Mountains tilted. The distance roared in her ears and clouds came like giant hands across the sun.

Still further out, dust lifted in waves as if trying to escape the barren ground and reach the fertile highlands. And she saw them.

Waiting for her.

She heard the radio, she saw the crisp white uniform with maroon trim, immaculate as ever despite the dust. Ellie did not question why they had come, or how. They had walked across two decades to meet her here, in the lee of a storm.

42

The police bring Baptist back, the fat red man with two African policemen. Baptist's legs are not broken but he stumbles, his eyes are swollen like black eggs. He smells of choo and sweat. You are crouching in the hedge, not meaning to be there, but the police car came and so you hid. The fat red man has a gun on his hip, he is the head policeman, and takes something out of his pocket and gives it to Dr McMullen. The paperweight.

'Little shit stole it,' he says. 'He has managed to tell us that there was a letter under it. We assume from your wife. But what it said or where it is, he just won't say. He's silent as a safe. And God knows I've tried to crack him.'

Baptist does not speak to you again, he does not speak to Rosa. She says, 'He is troubled, but the Lord will heal him.' But the Lord did not save Baptist's babies and he will not save Baptist.

You bury the letter under the sacred tree, the soft dark earth forming crescents under your fingernails. You bury the letter in the ground and bury the guilt in your heart.

43

They kneel down. Somewhere there is thunder. God is moving his furniture. But there is no God. There is no one to pray to. Rosa reaches up and takes her hand. Ellie knows Rosa is not there, knows she is a ghost, that she died in her village with her children and her grandchildren around her, with her cow and her small corn field, with August- ine's university diploma framed on the wall next to Jesus. But her hand is familiar, her hand comforts. So Ellie kneels between them.

Baptist is speaking in Kiluhya and Ellie cannot understand. She listens instead to the land, to the small sounds that are otherwise not heard. A grasshopper, a wasp, a bird. Looking up, she sees Pious. In his red hat, he is leaning on his shovel watching the sky. The clouds come, they arrive, as prayed for.

44

The rains have washed away Mum's garden at the house in Kabete. The irises and black-eyed Susans lie half-buried in the muddy stream at the bottom of the hill. You have rescued a few, with the roots intact, and are replanting them in a flower bed by the front door. A car pulls into the driveway. You look up and see your father. You think to run away but he has flowers in his hand, yellow roses.

'Hello,' he says.

You say nothing.

'Is your mother here?'

You shake your head. You are alone, she has gone with Gus, in a new dress.

He steps toward you, you step back.

He looks down at the flowers or his shoes.

He takes a rose from the others and hands it to you.

'Here,' he says. His hand trembles. The rose trembles.

You hesitate.

'Please take it.' His eyes are on yours. 'Please, Eleanor.'

You obey. He should go now, but he

doesn't. He stands there, wanting.

'Do you like living here?'

'Yes.'

'And school? Is school — are you happy at school?'

'Yes.'

Why doesn't he leave?

And then he suddenly leans down and pulls you to him. You can smell him, aftershave and whisky, the softness of his red sweater against your cheek. You hear him take in a breath, sharply, as a swimmer needing air. He is holding you against him, his hands lock into your hair. You are rigid with terror, waiting for his hands to spin and slap, for stinging skin.

He looks at you and quickly steps back. And turns away. He makes a small noise, a soft animal noise. He lifts the roses to his face.

'Tell her I came,' he says.

He gives you the roses and gets in his car and drives away.

45

The earth around her absorbs the rain. The rain has shuttered away the rest of the world and only this place remains. She has understood something Baptist said. Pray for forgiveness, he said. There is so much to forgive, so much to be forgiven.

She is kneeling.

★ ★ ★

My father died alone in that shitty room while children threw stones at his window, taunting him. He gathered his memories of me. There were so few. He thought of me, tried to imagine me, who I am now. As if I might walk through the door and quietly sit beside him.

Dying, he wished me to have everything of his, even if it was nothing: money, old papers. But it was *everything*, I see now, he was trying to tell me the truth, part of it. The only part that matters.

The words trembled on his lips but the words and the sentiment they expressed did not bring the African sun to the cold Scottish north or keep a burning plane in the sky or make him less afraid. The words would not make Helen stay or tarnish whisky's lustre or remove the fear from his daughter's eyes. The words were not a spell that could be cast to make the world a good and happy place.

When he was buried the worms were slow to acquire a taste for him. The whisky made them drunk, and the flesh, saturated with so much unspoken, was difficult to digest.

★   ★   ★

I am all that is left of my father.

I reach for the photograph of him as a small boy on the dock in Dar es Salaam. I have kept it on this journey.

And I see. Instead of leaving he is arriving. In this new country he runs barefoot in long grass and chases the dimpled light of the forest. Loved, laughing.

I invent his voice.

The stories he tells me of his life, the words weave a cloth that binds me and anchors me. The words are my way home to Peter who waits at the kitchen table and loves so patiently.

What we share of ourselves, what we speak and give is not enough. But we are only the dust of stars and it is all we have to keep from blowing away.

We do hope that you have enjoyed reading this large print book.

Did you know that all of our titles are available for purchase?

We publish a wide range of high quality large print books including:
Romances, Mysteries, Classics
General Fiction
Non Fiction and Westerns

Special interest titles available in large print are:
The Little Oxford Dictionary
Music Book
Song Book
Hymn Book
Service Book

Also available from us courtesy of Oxford University Press:
Young Readers' Dictionary
(large print edition)
Young Readers' Thesaurus
(large print edition)

For further information or a free brochure, please contact us at:
Ulverscroft Large Print Books Ltd.,
The Green, Bradgate Road, Anstey,
Leicester, LE7 7FU, England.
Tel: (00 44) 0116 236 4325
Fax: (00 44) 0116 234 0205

Other titles published by
The House of Ulverscroft:

SAFE HARBOUR

Janice Graham

As Canon of the Parisian cathedral of St John's, Crispin Wakefield has attracted a devoted following, but also the jealousy of his Dean. And the expensive indulgences of his wife and daughters are threatening financial ruin. Into this turmoil steps Julia Kramer, international actress and childhood friend from Crispin's family home back in Kansas. With her partner Jona frequently away, Julia is drawn into the cocoon of Crispin's family and his beloved cathedral. Deeply indebted, Julia uses her celebrity and wealth to promote Crispin's career. When Jona's business dealings lead him into deadly waters, Julia turns to Crispin for support, igniting vicious gossip . . .

A ROPE OF SAND

Elsie Burch Donald

A chance encounter in a French town brings dark memories flooding back to fifty-five-year-old Kate. As a student in the 1950s, she'd been one of five girls from Sweet Briar College, Virginia, to take a life-changing grand tour of Europe. Flung headlong into the dangerous freedom of the old world, Kate and her friends giddily soak up all that's on offer. When, one by one, three intriguing but very different young men latch on to the party, what seems to be a privileged and sophisticated clique is formed. But nobody is quite as they appear, and as facades crumble, the grand tour will prove eye-opening in ways the girls couldn't possibly have imagined.

THE RECKONING

Patricia Tyrrell

In a phonebooth beside a dusty Arizona highway, fifteen-year-old Cate listens in on yet another conversation between Les and her mother. But this is no ordinary parental discussion, for the woman hasn't seen her daughter since she was three years old, and the man is the homeless drifter who abducted her from beside her sleeping parents over a decade ago. Now Les has finally decided that Cate should go home. But how will Cate cope with learning to love a mother she can't remember? How will her English mother square the memories of her three-year-old daughter with the hard-bitten, poorly educated and cynical teenager? And what will happen when Cate's awful secret is revealed?

KITH & KIN

Stevie Davies

Mara and Frankie are cousins and best friends, growing up in the stifling atmosphere of Swansea in the Fifties, within an extended family that thrives on gossip, petty feuds and innuendo. Mara is a difficult but loved child whilst Frankie is rebellious, fired by an intense emotional hunger. The two develop a strange mutual dependence in which love, jealousy, hate and rivalry intermingle. They come of age in the Sixties — a decade in which notions of family and kinship are being overturned in favour of 'free love', sexual experimentation and social revolution. But that dream turns sour and a bitter battle of wills results . . .

LINDBERGH'S LEGACY

Katy Hayes

1926, on the south west coast of Ireland, in the aftermath of the bloody civil war: Marie-Rose O'Brien is about to give birth to her first child, as her handsome police sergeant husband, Cormac, patrols an uneasy peace. Shortly after the birth of baby Michael, the young family witness Charles Augustus Lindbergh's first flight across the Atlantic, as his plane passes over Ireland. Inspired by this, and fascinated by Lindbergh and all that he stands for, Marie-Rose tries to instil a sense of adventure in her son. It is this ambition, along with the pride he inherits from his father, which is set to run through the generations to come . . .

THE MEMORY STONES

Kate O'Riordan

Nell Hennessy left rural Ireland at sixteen to have her daughter, Ali. In over thirty years, she has never returned. Now she lives an uncluttered, elegant life in Paris, enjoying her independence, only broken from time to time by her married lover, Henri. Until a phone call shatters the peace of her carefully constructed world . . . Her daughter and granddaughter may be in grave danger and Nell can no longer avoid the inevitable. She must return to her childhood home. But what prevented Nell making that journey before? And how has the unspoken impinged on the lives of four generations of women?